Hilary McKay's
Fairy Tales

Illustrated by Sarah Gibb

MACMILLAN CHILDREN'S BOOKS

First published 2017 by Macmillan Children's Books
an imprint of Pan Macmillan
20 New Wharf Road, London N1 9RR
Associated companies throughout the world
www.panmacmillan.com

ISBN 978-1-4472-9229-6

Text copyright © Hilary McKay 2017
Illustrations copyright © Sarah Gibb 2017

The right of Hilary McKay and Sarah Gibb to be identified as the
author and illustrator of this work has been asserted by them
in accordance with the Copyright, Designs and Patents Act 1988.

1 3 5 7 9 8 6 4 2

A CIP catalogue record for this book is available from
the British Library.

Printed and bound by CPI Group (UK) Ltd, Croydon CR0 4YY

Contents

Introduction

Of course these are not *my* fairy tales; they are everyone's fairy tales, and have been for many years. Hundreds in the case of *The Pied Piper of Hamelin*, and thousands in the case of *Rumpelstiltskin*. They are our living heritage, true fairy gold, except these stories do not disappear at sunset. Their day still shines. The best of them are well and flourishing, in schools and libraries, homes and playgrounds, just as much as they are with historians and universities.

They live because they are so strong. They have withstood the years. Countries and rulers have come and gone, revolutions and wars have redrawn the old lines across Europe and beyond, forests have been felled, the wolves have all but vanished . . . and yet still their magic holds. Whoever has walked through a shadowy landscape, listening for the footsteps behind, has travelled with Red Riding Hood through the forest. Those far from home know the exile of the Swan Brothers. And I do not suppose there are many people reading this who have not speculated on the hazards of glass slippers, gingerbread houses, shiny red apples, and the problems of being caught out after midnight when you have been well warned that at the stroke of twelve, with no second chances, the party will be over.

With the help of friends and family, I chose ten stories out of dozens. Here is lovely Rapunzel, free from her tower, although perhaps not so free from her fears; Rumpelstiltskin, because all my life I have been troubled by the injustice with which he was treated; brave, loyal Elsa, who wove the nettles in silence for seven long years; Cinderella, who so much deserved her fairy godmother, and the twelve dancing princesses, who drove the old king to distraction by wearing through their slippers every night. (Which sounds like something he could have made less fuss about, until you do the maths: well over four thousand pairs of slippers a year. Satin slippers too!)

And, of course, there are still many questions. What did Hansel and Gretel say to their father when they finally made it home? What happened in Hamelin after the children vanished? Why did the Piper's son steal the pig? And how could Snow White have left those seven kind dwarves? Perhaps she never quite did.

It was exhausting and wonderful to write this book. I walked miles through forests. I watched swans and skies. I read and read. I studied maps and silks and brocades. I visited salt marshes and windmills. And now, here at last, is the finished collection, and I hope it works. Because if ever I wrote a book with love, it is this one!

Hilary McKay

1

The Tower and the Bird

or

Rapunzel

The tower stood on a small rise in the middle of the forest. It looked a little like a squat, dark windmill without its sails, or the monstrous chimney of some cold furnace. It was built of dark stone; reddish black and smelling of iron. Even on the brightest of days it was a menacing presence. And at night it loomed like a deliberate insult inked against the stars.

Grass and thorn bushes grew at the base of the tower, but the deer from the forest did not graze there. Nothing ever moved on the tower mound except for the scuttling witch.

The forest lapped all around, a green ocean of

trees. Great carved oaks and airy maples. Tall, sweet-scented pines. Rust-red streaks of hurrying squirrels. Many bright birds.

Jess and Leo always noticed birds because their mother loved them so much. 'They are so brave,' she said, 'and so fragile, and so quick and bright.'

Jess and Leo preferred dogs for company. Dogs who would come on adventures all day, and sleep on your bed all night. Their father, the Prince, loved his old white horse.

'But birds suit Mother,' Jess and Leo agreed, and so they looked out for the first swallow and counted the storks' nests on the rooftops in the village, and they saw the bird in the cottage window.

It was a small thing, green with a yellow head, hunched on its perch in a miniature cage. Three cats sat underneath, watching. The sight made Jess boil with indignation.

'We should steal it,' she said, 'and set it free. It's cruel!'

'We don't have to steal it,' said Leo, reasonably. 'There's other ways of getting things. Perhaps they would sell it.'

'We haven't any spare money. I suppose we could ask at home.'

'They haven't any spare either,' said Leo. And it was true that at the palace there was just enough money

to manage very carefully and not one penny extra for anything else. 'But it doesn't matter because I've still got my silver coin.'

Leo's silver coin had been a birthday present two years before, too rare and special to spend. Jess looked at him in admiration as he pulled it out of his pocket. Never could she have kept it for two days, never mind two years.

'We could ask,' she said. But asking wasn't easy. No one answered their knocks on the cottage door.

'We'll keep trying,' said Leo. And they did, for days and days, taking turns to go and knock and wait.

The bird hardly moved, and neither did the cats.

It was Jess who finally got a reply.

'Three silver coins!' she said, arriving breathless at the palace one evening. 'Three! We'll *have* to steal it!'

'Who told you three?' demanded Leo.

'The old man at the door, and the old woman behind him. "You're from the palace!" they said when they saw me. "Three's nothing to you!"'

'They must think we're rich.'

'I offered them one silver coin, and they laughed. "And your father a prince!" they said.'

'He's a poor prince! He's a writer. You should have told them that.'

'I did. They just shrugged. What can we do, Leo?'

'We've got one silver coin; we can earn some more. We've earned money before.'

They earned a second silver coin, one copper penny at a time, running errands for the sellers at the market-place. It took a week, such a long week that at the end of it Jess sold the green-and-gold bangle that was her most precious thing. That made three silver coins, and they brought the bird home in triumph and carried it to their mother.

'It's a yellowhammer,' said their mother. 'A poor little yellowhammer, half frightened to death.'

'Well, he needn't be frightened any longer,' said Jess jubilantly. 'We're going to open the door of the cage now!'

But the open door made no difference to the small hunched bird, and when they reached in to try and lift him, he panicked and fluttered away from their hands, beating his green wings against the bars of the cage until they thought he might break them. And he was no better the next day, or the next.

'All that work we did for him,' said Leo. 'And Jess's bangle and my silver coin! What a waste!'

'He's been in the cage so long, it's all the world he knows,' said the children's mother.

'Be patient,' agreed their father.

'We have been patient!' said Jess. 'We've been patient for nearly three days! How long can a person be patient for?'

'Much longer than that,' said her father.

The dark tower in the forest was a prison. There was a girl in the room at the top. It was a small round room, one window, no door. No light at night. No fire in winter. Nothing that might shine from the window and show a sign of life. A small bed, a wooden chair and an empty table.

The girl had been there for as long as she could remember. Her name was Rapunzel.

Time passed very slowly.

The tower was held together by the witch's spells, and it was she who kept Rapunzel captive there. She was the only person in Rapunzel's life, and Rapunzel was the only person in hers. Once a day, sometimes less often, the witch arrived with food. Rapunzel had never been so hungry nor so lonely that she did not dread those visits.

First the voice below:

'Rapunzel! Rapunzel! Let down your hair!'

For the witch climbed the tower by means of a rope hung from the window, and that rope was Rapunzel's long, long, soft golden hair.

The witch's hands as she climbed, clawing and groping; her weight like a swinging stone; her panting breath as she clambered over the sill.

'Smile, girl,' she would say. And Rapunzel would

smile, because what else could she do?

There were hardly any words between them. The witch would grumble, 'Here you sit. Idle as a princess. A fine life, dreaming. Dreaming while I work!'

Rapunzel would smile again. No use to reply. All the replies had been given years and years ago.

'Since you were a baby, waited on hand and foot. If you could see where I brought you from. Your father gave you up for a handful of herbs. Stolen herbs! Stolen from my garden! Have you nothing to say?'

Rapunzel shook her head.

'Your mother sent him thieving. A fine pair! But they gave you to me. Eighteen years ago. Lucky for you they did. Dead and gone and forgotten now. Dead and gone.'

'Yes,' whispered Rapunzel.

'There's bread, there's cheese, there's radishes. An apple and an egg.'

'Thank you.'

'Tomorrow, then; I'll be back tomorrow. Stand steady while I climb down.'

Then it was over.

That was how it was in the tower when the witch came.

But the moment the witch left, a robin alighted on the windowsill. Then swallows from under the eaves. Glossy jackdaws with silver eyes. A rainbow of finches. All that had frozen inside Rapunzel at the arrival of

the witch melted when the birds came back. They were her company; the only living things that could reach her. They made her laugh out loud, and she learned to whistle back to them, repeating their calls, and then she learned to sing. Rapunzel sang often, and her voice was clear and sweet, like a silver flute over the tree tops.

Rapunzel was singing at the tower window when the Prince came riding through the forest.

That first time he passed by without seeing the tower, and although he heard Rapunzel's song, he did not search for the singer. But at night Rapunzel's voice echoed through his dreams, and the next day he went again, and this time he followed the sound until he saw the tower rising through the trees, and a glint of brightness at the window that was Rapunzel's hair. He would have hurried forward, but at that moment there was a movement at the base of the tower, a dark figure and the rasping voice of the witch.

'Rapunzel! Rapunzel! Let down your hair!'

And then, to the Prince's astonishment, a silky golden braid fell from the high window, and the dark figure grasped it and began to scrabble and heave herself upwards, with her basket on her back.

The Prince stepped back into the shadow of the trees, and held his horse's head to keep it quiet, and waited, wondering.

Presently the golden hair was lowered again, and the witch reappeared at the window. A minute later and she was back on the ground. The Prince stood motionless while she gathered herself together and shuffled out of sight, and then he stepped out from between the trees and called, 'Rapunzel! Rapunzel!'

'Oh!' he heard a soft voice exclaim, and then Rapunzel looked out of the window.

This was the first time that she and the Prince saw

each other. The Prince did not climb the tower that day, nor the next, nor the next. But one day he did, and then he stood gazing around the bare little room, and at Rapunzel's pale face and frightened eyes, and he said, 'Rapunzel, let me help you out of here.'

'Oh no!' said Rapunzel. 'Oh no! How could I leave?'

'Easily, I'll bring a rope.'

'A rope?'

'A ladder, then. Or I'll wrap you in my cloak and lower you down.'

Rapunzel shook her head, half smiling, half bewildered. The little room was her only world. The ground looked impossibly distant. And even if she reached it, what then? To step away from the tower, to venture under the huge trees, exposed beneath the enormous sky, out into an empty world where she knew not one single friendly person.

'You know me,' said the Prince.

'The witch would be so angry.'

'Let her be.'

'She would rage,' said Rapunzel, trembling.

'I'd keep you safe.'

'She loves me too. She would weep.'

'Loves you!' exploded the Prince angrily. 'She has you prisoner here!'

'I should have to leave the birds.'

'Rapunzel! Dear, gentle, lovely Rapunzel, the birds

aren't bound to this tower. They're free to go where they please. The birds will come with you.'

But still Rapunzel shook her head, and gazed out of the window and said, 'I can't. You'd better go now.'

'I'll go,' said the Prince, 'but I'll be back. Every day until you change your mind. Don't you know I love you, Rapunzel? Come with me! Come with me now!'

But she shook her head, and could not speak.

He rode away as the sun was setting, and Rapunzel watched as the trees closed around him, and she cried aloud, 'Oh my Prince!'

But she also said, 'I daren't. Down there. Out there. Under that sky. And the witch. I couldn't. I can't! I can't! I can't!'

'Can't what?' demanded a voice from below, so suddenly that Rapunzel jumped and looked down from the window and gasped, 'Oh, it's you!'

'Let down your hair, Rapunzel!' ordered the witch, and it seemed to Rapunzel that she grasped even more fiercely than usual as she climbed and climbed faster than ever before, and panted more hotly and heavily as she lurched through the window. And the moment she stood on the floor, she said, 'Yes, it's me! Who else would it be? And what can't you do? Tell me what you've been up to, miss!'

'N-n-n-nothing,' stammered Rapunzel.

'Nothing? Then why are you blushing so red?'

'I'm not; it's just that the sun has grown warm.'

'Warm! Then why are you trembling, girl?'

'It's just that the wind is so cold.'

'I don't believe you! What are you hiding?' The witch glared around the bare little room, and then suddenly pounced and shrieked. 'WHERE DID THIS CLOAK COME FROM?'

Rapunzel stared in horror. The Prince's cloak! The Prince's green-and-gold riding cloak, thrown carelessly over the chair.

'Who has been here?' screamed the witch. 'Tell me! TELL ME!'

'The Prince!' whispered Rapunzel. 'The Prince.'

'The Prince! A prince! A *man* has been in here!'

'He . . . he . . . wanted to help me.'

'And how did he get here, girl? Tell me that!'

'The only way,' whispered Rapunzel.

'He climbed my rope? My golden rope?'

'Not yours,' said Rapunzel. 'Not yours!'

'You dare say that!'

Something flashed silver in the air, and the witch was holding a knife. She seized Rapunzel's great shining braid, and even as Rapunzel begged, 'No!' the witch tore and hacked with the blade until she held it in her hand.

'Mine now!' she jeered, sludge-grey tears rolling down the ancient leather of her cheeks. 'Mine forever! Mine!'

'Why did you do that?' cried Rapunzel. 'Why?'

The witch did not reply. She was knotting the cut end of Rapunzel's braid round the bed frame. When it was fast, she flung the length of it down the tower. Then she grasped the top in her hands, and swung herself over the sill.

The window was empty. Rapunzel closed her eyes in despair and disbelief and leaned her forehead against the cold wall. But only for a moment. Even as she sighed, the witch reappeared, reached into the room, clutched her wrist in her iron-strong fingers and dragged.

Over the sill she hauled Rapunzel. Out of the window, bruising her on the stone. The hair rope jerked, but the witch's knot held, and the witch's grip held too. Down they went together, grazing and sliding, and at the foot of the tower the witch let go.

'Run!' she ordered. 'Run far! Run fast!'

Rapunzel stood quite still.

'Run!' screamed the witch. 'Run, before I come after you! Run before I kill you! Run and never come back!'

Stumbling, half stunned, Rapunzel ran. She ran until she could no longer hear the witch's voice. Then she turned and looked back at the tower.

Rapunzel had lived in the tower for eighteen years, and now, for the first time, she saw it. Black it stood, wreathed in witchcraft, terrible against the evening sky, her hair still falling from the window. It made Rapunzel sick and faint to see it there. She turned away then, and she did not look back again.

But the witch climbed the golden rope back into the tower room, and she pulled it up after her and waited.

At dawn came the Prince, full of plans and promises, and he noticed nothing wrong, not even when the birds gathered around him, swooping and calling.

'*Rack! Rack! Rack!*' cried the blackbird, while the robin stood in his path.

'By your leave,' said the Prince, stepping round him, polite and unheeding, and he came to the tower and called.

'Rapunzel, Rapunzel! Dear Rapunzel! Lovely Rapunzel, let down your hair!'

So down for the last time came the rope of golden hair, and the Prince climbed swiftly to the window . . . and he was expected.

'Ha!' said the witch. 'Ha! Now I have you!'

'Where is she?' demanded the Prince, as soon as he understood. 'Rapunzel! What have you done with her? Tell me, old witch!'

'I'll tell you,' said the witch, the knife in her hand. 'I'll tell you! She's gone. Gone, and I'll never see her again! Gone, and you'll never see her again! Gone, and she won't come back, and she was mine, mine, mine!'

'No!' cried the Prince, rushing to the window. And he leaned out from it and called, 'Rapunzel! Rapunzel!'

'No use you crying,' said the witch. 'You took her! You lost her, and what'll I live for? Now fly after her if you can!'

She flung her weight against him, her whole dark weight of misery and evil and viciousness and hate, and out of the window hurtled the Prince, and from the whole height of the tower he plunged, head first. There were thorn bushes growing where he fell, and their branches broke his fall, and so he was not killed. But their thorns pierced his eyes.

The pain was like red fire.

Blinded, the Prince crawled, low along the ground, until he summoned the strength to drag himself to his feet. Then his horse, Seren, came to meet him and waited while he mounted.

'My good Seren; my brave Seren,' murmured the Prince.

Seren had been just in time. They had hardly moved a few yards into the trees when they heard the witch scream, and, before the scream had ended, another sound and worse.

Flesh and bones, breaking against stone, and then a great groaning rumble that shook the whole forest.

And afterwards, silence.

The Prince guessed then that the witch had jumped to her death, and he shuddered until he felt his own bones would break as well, and he could not move, and neither could his white horse. It was not until a robin sang from out of the trees in front of them that they found they could step forward.

One step, and then another, very slowly at first.

Now for the Prince, with his pierced eyes, the world was all darkness, but it was not so for Seren. Nor for the robin. All that day, the robin led the way through the forest, and the white horse followed. When night came they rested, and at dawn they travelled again.

This was the pattern for many days and nights, until at last there came a morning when the Prince heard the sudden flutter of the robin's wings as it flew by his face, and a lovely voice calling, 'Robin! Robin!'

'Rapunzel!' cried the Prince, and then she saw him.

That was how the Prince and Rapunzel came together again, and they clung to each other and laughed and wept and asked, 'Is it you? Is it you, at last? I thought I should never see you again!'

For, astonishingly, the Prince found that when their tears were brushed away, he could see once more.

He could see! The blue sky, the white horse, the robin on the green grass, and Rapunzel, smiling in his arms.

So the Prince and Rapunzel went back to his home, and they were married, and they had children.

Twins: Jess and Leo.

◇

Jess and Leo knew nothing of how their parents had met. They only knew they were as free as birds to wander the countryside and the marketplace and the small shabby palace that was home. The village school taught them to read, their father taught them to ride and climb, and their mother taught them to sing. One day they brought home a yellow-and-green bird in a woven cage, and opened the door and waited.

But it was a long time before the bird looked out.

Longer still until he left the cage, and even then he didn't go far, nor for long. Every few minutes he was back inside again.

'He wants to be a prisoner,' said Leo.

'He doesn't,' said Jess, and took the cage away. That didn't help either. The little bird hopped back to where it had stood. He put himself into an invisible cage, until they gave him the real one again.

'I don't understand,' said Leo.

And Jess said, 'Neither do I.'

◇

But their mother looked at the little bird, and she understood. She too had been a prisoner, and she too was free. And now she was the Prince's wife, and the mother of two children; but still she was also Rapunzel.

Rapunzel in the tower.

The tower, the tower, the round bare room. The darkness of the forest at night, and the moonlight on the walls. The chill and the wind and the scudding clouds outside. The cold iron smell of wet stone. The sheets of rain that splattered on the floor. The bliss of sunlight. The huge silences before a storm. Her lost prison. Her lost world. There were moments when she ached for it so much she would have gone back in a heartbeat, just to be home again. It was as if the tower was still holding her. She saw it in her dreams, an ink-black shape blotted against the sky.

'It's gone,' said the Prince. 'Dear Rapunzel, it's gone. It fell when the witch fell. I felt the earth shake with the weight of the stone.'

'I know,' said Rapunzel.

'Try to believe it.'

◇

'Try to believe it,' Rapunzel told the little bird one bright morning. It was out of its cage, just then, perched on the top and preening. Watching, it suddenly struck Rapunzel that this was good. It was no longer hunched and quiet. It looked at her and chirped.

Then Rapunzel remembered something from a long time ago. The small, silly song of a yellowhammer, and the first skill she had learned from the birds.

'Mother!' exclaimed Leo, coming in with Jess. 'I didn't know you could whistle like that!'

'Do it again!' begged Jess.

Rapunzel laughed, and whistled again, and the bird

on the cage cocked his head, winked at her with a bright, dark eye, and stretched a wing consideringly. Then suddenly, with no fuss at all, it rose from the top of the cage, circled the room, and flew out of the open window.

'Oh! Oh!' cried Jess and Leo.

'Listen!' said their mother.

From the top of a birch tree a song came winging back to them. It was the small, silly song of a yellowhammer, swinging in the sunlight.

Rapunzel ran to the garden and gazed and gazed.

And at last there was nothing but sky above her, and sunlight and birdsong and small white clouds against the blue.

And there was no cage and no tower and no shadow anywhere to blot out the light.

And so then they all lived happily.

Ever after.

2

Straw into Gold
or
Rumpelstiltskin

There was a salt marsh under an enormous sky. It was a bare, wild place of creeks and mudflats, sea lavender and reed beds. It was the home of wading birds and seals and gulls. For years, a small creature had lived there too. Root dark, reed thin, perhaps half the height of a man, perhaps less. Not an imp, nor a boggart, nor an elf. Something of that kind, but without their charm or mystery. Without their easy magic too. He was a hob. A plain, scuttling hob, with a husky, piping voice.

◇

Before the hob came to the marsh, he had lived inland, where there were barley fields and windmills and fat

meadow sheep. Amongst the meadows was a village, with cottages and farms and apple orchards. In one of those orchards had been a low brick building where, long before, a farmer had kept turkeys. The old turkey house, overgrown to the roof with a thorny, pale pink rose, made a home for the hob.

The hob had no name; or if he had, he had never heard it told. The village people had no name for him either. They called him 'Eh up!' 'Yon fella', 'Now then!' and 'Li'l chap.' He worked for them, and they paid him in barley loaves, bowls of milk, fallen apples, hot broth in wintertime, a three-legged stool and a woollen patchwork blanket. In return he picked stones from the fields, cleaned the stables and sheds, swept the yards, sat up at night beside sick beasts, brewed cures from herbs, and spun the wool from the fleeces of the fat sheep into great, smooth hanks of yarn.

The hob was good at spinning. He had a little wooden spinning wheel, cut down to suit his size. When he wasn't at his farm work, he sat in the doorway of the old turkey house with his wheel, and he sang sometimes; thin, reedy songs of his own thoughts:

Fair days such fair days never seen such fair days
With light on the barley
When the wind blows.

One day the hob was singing a song such as this, when a woman went past with a child. The hob watched them. He always watched children, especially very small ones. They seemed less remote to him than grown people did. This child, a girl in a blue dress, was of the age when children learn to speak. She was pointing to things and naming them.

When the hob realized this, he put his hand on the wheel to stop the spinning and listened.

'Sky,' said the child, gazing upwards.

And the woman said, 'Yes. Sky.'

'Stick,' said the child, stooping to pick up a fallen birch twig, and again the woman agreed.

''Onkey!' The child pointed in glee at a nodding grey head at a gate.

'Donkey,' said the woman, smiling.

'Donkey, donkey!' said the child, nodding so much

like the donkey that the hob's beechnut pointy face twisted into a smile. The girl saw the smile and laughed back and spoke again.

A name.

The hob's eyes grew wide. His mouth fell open. His heart pounded so hard he felt faint and fearful. He was fearful in case the child was mistaken. He fixed his eyes on the woman. She nodded tranquilly to the child and added, 'Spinning! Straw into gold!'

That was a saying they had in those parts: 'Straw into gold', a sort of joke. A sort of impossible wish or hope.

The woman and the little girl passed on, but just as they turned the corner out of sight, the girl looked back over her shoulder, straight into the face of the hob, and she said his name again.

Now the hob's days were different. He had a name. In the night he murmured it, and hugged it to himself like a great treasure. In the day his steps were bolder. When his work was done he walked up and down the village street looking about himself.

This was all because of knowing his name.

The hob's spinning now became supreme. He worked with a new, wild energy. There came a day when he turned his wheel so fast that there was no combed fleece left in the village to be spun. Yet the hob still burned with his bold new eagerness. What could he spin? He looked around his little turkey-house home. Then he remembered, for the first time since he had heard them, the words of the woman with the child.

Straw into gold.

The hob turned to his bed and gathered a bunch of barley straw.

Then in secret, and with great difficulty and some pain in his hands, the hob spun a new thread. He spun the barley straw into a thick solid thread of pure bright gold. When it was finished he wound the new thread into a shining acorn-sized ball and held it in his hand. It glowed like a miniature sun on the hob's dark palm.

Gold was no part of the hob's life. He had his milk and his barley bread, his blanket and his rose. He had his name to murmur at night. He had no use for this little piece of gold, and yet he knew it was a wonder. So he took it into the village and walked up and down the street with it until he stumbled over a cart-rut in front of the village inn. He dropped the gold then, and it rolled away, and he crawled in the gutter, searching for it.

It was not often that people spoke to the hob, but now and then they did. As he scrabbled, a kindly voice asked, 'What you doing, li'l chap?'

'I dropped my gold,' said the hob.

'Your gold?'

'My piece of gold,' said the hob.

'Ha!' called the man to the group in front of the inn. 'They're paying the hob in gold now! What about that?'

Laughter broke over the hob and buffeted him.

'What you been up to in that orchard, then,' someone called to him, 'to be worth so much?'

'Spinnin',' said the hob.

'That must have been rare fleece!'

'Barley straw,' said the hob.

'You been spinning barley straw?'

'Spun it into gold,' said the hob proudly.

This time the laughter was a gale, and the men slapped their knees, and those that had heard called to those that had not, 'Come, listen to this!' and they said to the hob, 'Tell it again!'

'Spun straw to gold,' repeated the hob, looking from one huge laughing face to another. 'Barley straw.'

The landlord was amongst them now, with a great jug of barley beer and a fistful of mugs. 'That's a joke well worth a drink!' he said, squatting down to speak to the hob. 'There you go, li'l fella!'

The hob took his mug in two hands, and it was like a barrel to him and smelt like all the good things he had ever smelt, earth and barley and honey and new bread, all of them in one. It tasted like them too, and he drank it down, gulp by gulp, and wagged his head with the strong, good, dizzy feel of it, and wiped the foam on his fingers.

'And what would you have bought with your barley-straw gold?' asked a grinning face. 'What was it to be, my fine spinner?'

The hob shook his swimming head.

'Barley beer?' they asked him. 'A fine new hat? A riding mare? What do you lack, fella? What's your desire? What would you buy?'

The hob looked from one to the other. More questions than he had ever been asked in his life. His head buzzing with barley beer. What did he lack? A companion. A soul to work for. A voice to say his name.

'One thing?' asked a man, laughing.

'A child,' said the baffled, beer-swarmed, lonely hob.

'A child?' said the man, and all the laughter stopped. The world stopped.

'A child?' they repeated. And they asked each other, 'What would a creature like a hob want with a child? What have we kept amongst us?'

That was the end of the hob's days in the village, and the turkey house and the rose, and the barley bread and the bowls of milk. The hob's world was pulled apart by great men's hands, the rose torn up, the stool smashed, the walls demolished and the roof destroyed, and the hob himself sent running, scurrying, hobbling from the village, with hard words and stones following after him, and his spinning wheel strapped to his back.

He was outcast, and he had not the smallest understanding of why.

It was dark now all the time in the hob's world. Daylight made no difference to his darkness. He groped blindly forward into an empty nothingness. He felt no hunger, nor thirst, nor tiredness. He felt nothing but the road beneath his feet, until he came to the wall.

The wall barred his way. He could not pass it and so he dropped against it. For a long time he lay crumpled there, neither awake nor asleep.

Rain fell on him . . .

The hob did not die, and so he had to go on living.

He opened his eyes, and the sky was still there. Towering above him was a great, creaking windmill, red brick and white sails and long green grass at the foot. The spinning wheel lay tangled amongst the grasses.

Since the hob had to live, he had to eat. To eat, he had to work. Very slowly, with the wall to help him, he pulled himself to his feet, staggered round to the dark open door of the mill, found a broom and began to sweep the floor.

◇

The miller's daughter was named Petal, and it suited her. She was a round, soft blossom of a girl, golden-haired, pink-skinned, and as lazy as she was pretty. Petal drifted through her days, dreamily combing her long, smooth curls, smiling when the sunlight moved round to her chair, sleepily humming on the garden swing. She had a nice singing voice, but she never did anything useful except, now and then, a little spinning.

'You can spin sitting down,' said Petal.

The miller said, 'I never knew anyone do so little for so long!'

'Well, now you do,' said Petal.

'Big lass like you should be busy with all sorts!' said the miller. 'What's going to happen when you marry, my fine lady? Then who will keep the house?'

'Housemaids!' said Petal.

'And cook the food?'

'Kitchen maids!' said Petal.

'And mind the babies?'

'Nursemaids!' said Petal. 'Of course!'

'Then mind you marry a very rich man, our Petal!'

'I'll marry the King,' said Petal. 'He's rich enough!'

'Marry the King!' scoffed the miller. 'I'd like to see the King marry a girl like you!'

'Watch, then,' said Petal, 'and you will.'

The miller grunted with temper. He always lost his arguments with Petal; he had done all her life.

'There's a hob about,' he told her, changing the subject.

'Fancy,' said Petal, yawning.

'I've not seen it, but it's there. Sweeps the mill and does the stable. Brews cures from herbs. Cured the bay horse. I been leaving it porridge, and a coin now and then.'

'When the King comes,' said Petal, who had been smiling into her little looking glass and not listening to a word, 'tell him I'm here.'

'The King!' growled the miller. 'That'll be the day, when the King leaves his great palace in the middle of town to come out here by the marsh and knock on the mill-house door! You do have some ideas!'

'I do,' said Petal.

'You'll wait forever and a day!'

'A day will be enough,' said Petal. And as usual she was right and the miller was wrong, and the next day the King left his great palace in the town and came knocking on the mill-house door, his carriage having lost a wheel in the road outside, and he himself not wanting to stand around in the rain till it was mended.

So the King was shown into the mill-house parlour and handed a glass of the miller's best wine (which he ungratefully poured out of the window) while the miller ran upstairs to ask Petal how she knew.

'Knew what?' asked Petal, rolling dozily over in bed.

'Don't you notice nothing?' demanded the miller. 'We've got the King down there, sitting in the parlour!'

'Well then,' said Petal, 'tell him you've got a daughter as beautiful as the day, and she'll marry him soon as he's ready!'

'I don't know how he'll take that,' said the miller doubtfully.

'He'll be enchanted,' said Petal, but this time she was wrong. The King did not seem at all enchanted.

'Thoughtful of her,' he said, sounding completely uninterested, and he looked out of the window to see if his carriage was mended yet.

Petal, who had been listening over the banisters, now called, 'Father! Father!'

'What now?' asked the miller, hurrying back up the stairs.

'Tell the King,' said Petal, 'you've got a daughter as beautiful as the day, who can sing sweet as a bird, and she'll marry him any day he likes!'

'Astonishing,' said the King, when he heard this good news, and his eyes rolled with boredom to the ceiling.

'Father!' called Petal over the banister, once again. 'Father, come here!'

The miller groaned, but came.

'Tell the King,' said Petal, 'you've got a daughter as beautiful as the day and can sing sweet as a bird . . .'

'Yes, yes,' said the miller. 'I did.'

'. . . and can spin straw into gold!' said Petal.

'Straw into gold?' asked the miller, staring.

Petal nodded, bright-eyed and lovely in her pink dressing gown and fluffy slippers. 'And who will marry him,' she continued, 'whenever he asks!'

'Don't be daft, our Petal!' said the miller, coming to his senses. 'He'd have my head off for impertinence!

I'm not telling him that!'

'Not telling him what?' demanded the King, appearing suddenly in the parlour doorway.

'Ooh, Your Majesty!' squeaked Petal, blushing behind her silky gold curls as she retreated modestly back to her bedroom, clutching her dressing gown.

'Not telling him WHAT?' demanded the King of the unhappy miller.

'Only her nonsense,' said the miller.

'What nonsense?' snapped the King, icily regal.

'That she is as b-b-b-beautiful as the day and can s-s-s-sing sweet as a bird and can spin straw into g-g-g-g-g—'

'Spit it out, man!' roared the King.

'Gold!'

'*Gold?*'

'Yes,' agreed the miller, wishing he had never spoken, nor opened the door to the King, nor had a daughter either. 'And she'll m-m-m-marry you whenever you ask.'

'Will she now?' said the King thoughtfully. 'Hmm, I'd have to see the proof.'

◇

Petal. The hob heard her weeping, out in the barn.

The carriage was mended. The King was gone. The miller, sick of the whole awful business, had taken himself off into town. Petal was alone with her spinning

32

wheel and a bundle of straw and tears running down her cheeks.

'It's not fair!' she sobbed.

The hob had never seen her before, although he had heard her singing around the mill now and then. He crept up to the window and stared at her, speechless.

'I never thought he'd want it done!' said Petal. 'I just said it to make him look at me! I thought once he saw I was beautiful as the,' *sniff*, 'day, he'd marry me with no more fuss!'

She *was* beautiful. The hob sighed at such sadness from someone so lovely, and Petal heard him and looked up.

'Who are you?' she asked. 'The hob?'

The hob nodded.

'Did my father send you?'

The hob shook his head.

'I can't spin straw into gold. No one could.'

Something in the hob's stillness caught her attention. 'Could you?' she asked. 'You're clever, I hear. You cured the horse's cough.'

'That was flaxseed.'

'And my father's stiff back.'

'That was meadowsweet.'

'I think you could spin straw into gold!'

'No,' said the hob huskily.

'Then I could marry the King!'

'You don't want to,' said the hob.

'I do! Spin it for me, hob!'

The hob backed away.

'I'll give you my beads. My green glass beads.'

'I don't want your beads,' muttered the hob.

But she had already taken them off and looped them around his neck. 'Spin it!' she said. 'He's coming back in the morning!'

And because she was so lovely and her eyes so blue and her tears so silver, the hob went reluctantly to the spinning wheel and sat down. Then, with pain in his hands, he spun the bundle of straw into a length of golden thread.

'Is that all it made?' asked Petal when she saw.

'It weren't that much straw,' said the hob, and he scuttled away to nurse his aching hands before any more was asked of him.

◇

So he did not hear the relief of the miller when he came home, nor the astonishment of the King in the morning, nor Petal saying, smiling but modest, 'It weren't that much straw.'

'No,' said the King, looking at her thoughtfully. 'What's your name, girl?'

'Petal,' said Petal, bobbing a curtsy.

'You wouldn't deceive me, Petal?'

'Not me,' said Petal, with her fingers crossed

firmly behind her back.

'I should like you to spin a wagonload.'

'A wagonload?' repeated Petal.

'Why not?'

''Tisn't easy,' murmured Petal. 'There's not many girls could do it.'

'There's not many girls I'd marry,' said the King. 'I'll send the wagonload of straw and I'll be back in the morning to see my gold, unless . . .' He paused, and looked at Petal.

'Unless what?' asked Petal.

'Unless you've deceived me,' he said coldly.

◇

That night, the hob spun again. He spun until his hands twisted with pain. What else could he do? There were Petal's tears. There was Petal's frightened pleading. There was Petal's blue ring.

'I don't want your ring,' he'd said, looking at his twisted hands.

'You could thread it on the beads,' said Petal. And even as she spoke, she'd done it, and hung them back around his neck, and then there he was spinning, the hardest work he had ever done . . . but the straw was gold by morning. Bright golden thread.

◇

'A barnful,' said the King.

'Oh no,' said Petal.

'A barnful, if you haven't deceived me.'

'A barnful, then what?' asked Petal fearfully. 'Ten barns?'

'A barnful, and then we marry,' said the King.

'No more spinning?'

'No more spinning.'

'I don't know if I can.'

'You can if you haven't deceived me. If you have . . . well . . .'

Petal had lowered her eyes, but not before she saw the tiny gesture the King made with his hand.

'A barnful,' said the King, gentle as sunlight, 'and then no more spinning and happily ever after.'

◇

The hob had made up his mind. He wouldn't come. He wouldn't spin again. He would leave the mill and go far away, and never, ever return.

Petal was sobbing. Out in the barn with her spinning wheel, straw piled all around her.

'Spin it for me, hob,' she said.

'Too much.'

'I'm frightened.'

'Then run,' said the hob.

'Then I won't marry the King.'

'You don't want to.'

'I do,' said Petal. 'I do. I do. Spin it for me, hob. I gave you my ring. I gave you my beads. Spin it, and

I'll give you my first child.'

'No!' said the hob, drawing back.

'I promise.'

'Don't promise.'

'Too late. I've done it. The child is yours! I'll send word to the mill when it's born. Do you want a child, hob?'

'Yes,' said the hob longingly. 'I do.'

'Spin then, because I don't.'

◇

The thread that the hob spun that night in the barn was red gold, and when it was finished the hob knew he could never spin again. His hands were broken and bleeding, and for a long time he could hardly hold the broom to sweep the floors. Nevertheless, he kept them swept, and the stable clean, and meadowsweet tea brewed for the miller's stiff back. Petal and the King were married. Petal never visited the mill any more, but the miller would go to the palace. The hob heard him telling a farmer who came to the mill with a load of grain, 'Our Petal's the Queen at the palace!'

'Doing well?' asked the farmer.

'Doing grand,' said the miller. 'In silks and satins and diamonds.'

'And who takes care of the palace?'

'Housemaids,' said the miller.

'And cooks the food?'

'Kitchen maids,' said the miller.

'And will mind the child when it comes along?'

'Nursemaids, of course,' said the miller. 'Our Petal worked that one out long ago, and the child will be here next month. She sent a message.'

◇

Now the hob's days were filled with hope, and he began to prepare. His hands could no longer spin, but they were still clever. On the edge of the salt marsh he built himself a house, with walls of silver driftwood, a thatch of golden reeds, and purple sea lavender as far as the shining sea.

And although there was very little magic about the hob, when his house was finished he spun spells around it.

Then the day came when a message arrived at the mill with news of a child at the palace, a boy.

My boy, thought the hob with joy.

◇

Petal said, when the hob arrived at the palace, 'Did I say that?'

The hob nodded.

'I can't think why!'

'Straw spun into gold,' said the hob, holding out his hands. 'That was why.'

'But what has that to do with you?' asked Petal.

The hob looked at her.

'Everybody knows it was me who spun the straw into gold!' said Petal. 'Everybody! Even the King! A bundle. A cartload. A barnful.' Her voice was bright with laughter, but her eyes were frightened. 'It's a good thing the King isn't here,' she continued. 'What would he do to us both, if he heard your claim?'

'What would he do?' asked the hob, and flinched as she made a tiny movement with her hand.

'Anyway, what would a creature like you do with a child?' asked Petal.

'What do you do?' asked the hob.

'Me? Nothing,' said Petal. 'It's a poor thing. A poor sort of child. I think it looks like him.'

'And what does *he* do?'

'The King? Nothing,' said Petal. 'He thinks it looks like me.'

There was a long silence, broken by Petal.

'There are peacocks on the terrace,' she said, 'and deer in the park. I have silks and satins and velvets and furs. Diamonds by the dozen! There are dances and plays and masques and balls. It's a much better life than the mill.'

Petal fell silent again.

'And the King?' asked the hob.

'He's hardly here. He hunts far away.'

'Who cares for the child?'

'Nursemaids, I suppose,' said Petal. 'Not me. I don't care for it.'

'The King?' asked the hob.

Petal laughed. 'The King, care for a child?'

'It was a bargain,' said the hob. 'I should have the child, you said. For spinning the straw . . .'

'Hush!' said Petal.

'. . . to gold.'

'Listen, old hob, we'll make a new bargain. How about that?'

'The old one was good enough,' said the hob.

'Not for me,' said Petal, tossing her bright hair. 'So now then, whatsyourname . . . What *is* your name, hob?'

'My own,' said the hob.

'Tell me!'

'I won't!'

'You don't speak to me as you should to a queen. You should say "Ma'am" and bow low!'

'Ma'am,' said the hob, bowing very low, 'I've come for the child.'

'Spin me more gold!'

'I can't.'

'Tell me your name!'

'I won't.'

'Well then, be off!'

'A bargain's a bargain,' said the hob stubbornly.

'I want a new one!'

'I got nothing to bargain,' said the hob, 'with a fine lady like you.'

'You have your name,' said Petal. 'Listen! I guess your name, I keep the child.'

'Guess then,' said the hob.

'Balthazar!'

'No it's not. Give me the poor child! I'll care for him.'

'I need more guesses than that!' snapped Petal.

'How many?' asked the hob.

'Three.'

'Go on then. Guess two more.'

'Jackanapes!' said Petal.

'No it's not. Give me the poor child. I'll work for him.'

'Tomkins!' guessed Petal.

'No it's not,' said the hob. 'Give me the poor child. I'll love him.'

'I need more guesses!' said Petal. 'I need three guesses for three days!'

'Mistress Petal, Ma'am, Queen Petal?'

'What then?'

'Do you love the child?'

'Love it?'

'Aye.'

'I don't know what you are talking about,' said Petal sulkily.

'The child,' said the hob. 'I'll care for him. I'll work for him. I'll love him.'

'Three guesses for three days,' said Petal.

'Then you'll give me the child?' asked the hob.

'If I haven't guessed your name.'

'Do you promise?' asked the hob.

'Yes, I promise,' said Petal.

◊

The hob returned to the mill, swept the floors, cleaned the stable, bound the donkey's bad knee with a bundle of comfrey leaves to take out the swelling, ate his porridge and went out to his house on the marsh. Round and round the house he spun songs into spells.

◊

At the palace the next day, Petal was waiting.

'I asked the maids,' she said. 'The maids say your name is Charlie, and so do I.'

'The maids are wrong, and so are you,' said the hob.

'I asked at the stables. The lads say Robin, and so do I.'

'The lads are wrong, and so are you,' said the hob.

'The cook said William, and so did the butler, and so do I say William too.'

'Then you're all three wrong,' said the hob.

'There's still tomorrow,' said Petal.

'I'll be back tomorrow,' said the hob. 'Is the child well?'

'It wails in the night,' said Petal.

'Sing to it,' said the hob.

And Petal was suddenly furious, and she shouted after the hob, 'You are a hob! I'm the Queen!

Don't tell ME what to do!'

But the hob was already gone, back to the mill, and then out to the marsh, and Petal was left alone.

'I AM the Queen,' she said, sobbing with temper. 'And I WON'T be beaten by a hob!'

◇

That night the hob spun his spell, round and around the house on the marsh:

Let the thatch be thick and warm,
Let the walls withstand the storm,
Let the woven cradle hold
Fairer dreams than straw to gold.

Painted skies at morning light,
Stars like blossom through the night,
Salt-marsh music, sweet and wild,
All for Rumpelstiltskin's child!

Over and over, the hob spun his spell, alone on the salt marsh, and the wind caught his words and blew them out into the darkness, over the reeds, under the stars, and far, far away.

◇

'Ah!' said Petal.

◇

Then came the third day.

'Blackshanks!' said Petal, smiling under her long eyelashes at the hob.

'Not Blackshanks,' said the hob thankfully.

'Then,' said Petal, two guesses short of losing her child, her face dimpling with mischief, 'Hopeless! I would call you Hopeless!'

'Not Hopeless,' said the hob, and it was true. He was not hopeless. His eyes were shining with love and hope.

But Petal's eyes were shining too. Petal's eyes were dancing with pleasure. Petal pointed a pink finger at the hob and said:

'Your name . . .'

Laughter overcame her for a moment:

'Your name is . . .'

She doubled up with mirth:

'Your name is RUMPELSTILTSKIN!' cried Petal. 'RUMPELSTILTSKIN! RUMPELSTILTSKIN! YOUR NAME IS RUMPELSTILTSKIN!'

Right there, before her eyes, the hob tumbled, sank to the floor as his strength ran away, hunched into his arms, rocked with misery, puddled into grief.

Petal looked at him uncertainly, and then, after a moment or two, stepped carefully round him and left him alone.

◇

Round and round spun the world. Winter came and frost crackled in the reed beds. Summer brought the lazy seals. Wild geese came in autumn. The sea lavender was purple in the spring. The sails of the windmill turned. Moons waxed and waned, and the tides moved with them.

◇

Years passed.

◇

The boy arrived one autumn afternoon. He was not like his dead father, nor his mother. He was his own self, as brave as the sunlight on the reeds, as honest as the salt wind that blew across the marsh. When he came to the old house, he sat quietly by the open door and waited until at last he heard a movement from inside.

He said, 'I heard the story. Straw into gold. And your name. She told me.'

'Petal?' whispered the hob.

'My mother,' said the boy, and rubbed away a tear.

'She's gone?' asked the hob.

The boy nodded. 'She used to sing to me,' he said.

'She had a voice sweet as a bird, did Petal,' said the hob.

'The straw into gold. And your name. She was sorry. She told me where to find you. I promised her I would. She wanted you to know she was sorry that she tricked you.'

'No matter,' said the hob, his heart thumping with gladness. 'No matter. She sang to you. That's what you must remember.'

The boy lifted his head and looked around him.

'I used to dream dreams of a place like this. There was music there too.'

'That'd be the wind in the reed beds,' said the hob.

◇

So the afternoon passed. The hob and his boy sat together contentedly until the air grew cold. Then they built a fire of driftwood and it burned with small blue flames while above them, one by one, the stars opened like blossoms in the painted evening sky.

3

The Roses Round the Palace
or
Cinderella

There was the Prince, dark-haired and tall, intelligent and rich. He was a most royal prince; his blood was bright blue, and his throne was bright gold, and his crown was bright with rubies and sapphires and emeralds. Naturally he lived in a palace with gilded turrets and diamond-paned windows and banners streaming in the wind. Also roses, climbing the old stone walls to the balconies, with a smell so sweet that on still summer nights the scent rolled down the hill and over the little river and bathed the town in perfume.

There were many, many royal princesses who would have liked to marry the Prince.

There was Buttons, the palace boot boy, a great grumbler who said that the Prince made him feel shivery and the roses made him sneeze.

And there was Cinderella. But hardly anyone knew about her, as she lived so hidden away.

◇

Cinderella lived in a great dark kitchen at the bottom of a tall, narrow house. The kitchen was all flagstones and beetles and cobwebby rafters. At one end a heavy old door led into a little stone yard. At the other end was a fireplace as large as a cave. Steep steps came down from the rooms above. In those rooms lived Cinderella's family: her stepmother and stepsisters. Her own mother was dead, and her father's business had been in a city far away, until it failed. He had never understood that it failed. He stayed in the city, old and ill, with a memory like a dying fire. Sometimes, rarer and rarer times, it flamed into life, and he remembered he had a child named Cinderella. Then he came home and crept carefully down the steps into the kitchen to put his shaky old hand on Cinderella's brown silk hair and whisper, 'My dear. My dearest.'

Those times were so precious to Cinderella that they were worth the long grey stretches in between.

During the grey times, Cinderella would go for whole weeks without seeing her stepmother or stepsisters. She didn't mind a bit. She could hear them, and she thought that was more than enough. Their sharp, greedy voices called down the stairs, 'Cinderella! Cinder*ella!* CinderELLA! Pulley! Be quick!'

The pulley was a creaky old thing that swayed on ropes up and down a long shaft between the kitchen and the rest of the house. Cinderella, at intervals during the day, would load it with such things as breakfast, elevenses, lunch, tea and cakes, dinner, late supper, snacks and nibbles. Also ironed gowns, clean stockings, polished shoes, shining candlesticks, filled log baskets, loaded coal buckets, and a hundred other things.

In return, down to the kitchen would come empty dishes, grubby boots, tumbled bags of supplies from the market, and bundles of laundry, all to be dealt with by Cinderella as quickly as possible.

'You should run off,' advised Buttons, but Cinderella shook her head. She had nowhere to run to, and no shoes to run in, only tatty thin slippers with her toes peeping out of them. And anyway, her father might come back.

'You could leave him a message,' said Buttons, who had never met Cinderella's father.

'They'd never tell him.'

'Write it down.'

'His eyes find reading hard these days.'

'You'll just have to wait, then,' said Buttons, 'until something turns up.'

'That's what I think too,' said Cinderella cheerfully.

Meanwhile, things were not so bad, because Cinderella, as well as being very brave and very pretty, was very good at being happy with very small things. She admired the square of blue sky that made a roof to her little stone yard, and she enjoyed the flickering light on the rafters when the fire was alight in the hearth. On washing days she blew bubbles with soap suds and sent them sailing into the wind; on baking days she made plaited loaves and pastry roses; and every day she threw crumbs to the sparrows that waited on the doorstep.

It made no difference that when her stepmother and stepsisters caught her at these things they were dreadfully angry.

'Waste of bread!' they said, about the sparrows and the crumbs.

'Waste of soap!' they cried, about the bubbles.

'Waste of time!' they complained, about the plaited loaves and pastry roses. 'And it uses too much flour.'

Then the sparrows were chased away, and various methods of making Cinderella uncomfortable were invented, such as taking away the small kitchen rocking chair or the faded quilt that covered her bed in the alcove. Cinderella put up with the punishments quite calmly and did not stop blowing bubbles or making pastry roses or feeding the sparrows.

'It's worth it,' she told Buttons, when he climbed the yard wall to visit her.

'You could give up the baking,' said Buttons.

'Baking keeps me warm,' said Cinderella.

'Well then, the sparrows.'

'What, and leave them hungry?'

'Then the bubbles,' said Buttons,

'The first bubbles I ever blew flew over the wall and you saw them. Don't you remember how you followed them back to the kitchen door?'

'With the Prince's boots,' said Buttons.

'All muddy in a sack!' remembered Cinderella. 'And you were going to swish them in the river to try and get them clean!'

'Well, how was I to know what to do with boots?' asked Buttons.

'Lucky for you that I knew!' said Cinderella, smiling. And Buttons, although he didn't really approve of cheerfulness, had to agree. It *had* been lucky, and it still was lucky, because ever since that first day as a boot boy to the Prince he had brought a sack of the royal boots with him when he visited Cinderella. He didn't like polishing on his own, he said, and since Cinderella was so good at it, they did it together, Buttons doing the left boots, and Cinderella the right ones, and then all the extra left ones that Buttons hadn't finished, because she was by far the fastest at polishing.

And some people might have thought it wasn't fair, that Cinderella should have to do such a large amount of Button's work, as well as her own, but:

'It's worth it,' said Cinderella.

It *was* worth it, because with Buttons came all the news from the palace, from the banners above the turrets to the roses around the walls.

'Blooming things!' said Buttons. 'And the Prince never leaves them alone! He pushes them on people; that's what he does! This morning he heaved down a great bunch and shoved them up me nose! "Look!" he says. "Ruby red!"'

'Oh, how gorgeous!'

'"Smell!" he orders. "Perfumes of paradise!"'

'Lucky, lucky Buttons!' murmured Cinderella.

'"Touch!" he tells me. "Satin and silk!"'

'Mmm,' sighed Cinderella.

'And the next thing I know,' said Buttons indignantly, 'there was a thorn!'

'Well, roses have thorns.'

'Jabbed in my thumb!'

'But satin and silk!' remembered Cinderella.

'Stabbed!' said Buttons. 'Agony!'

'But perfumes of paradise!' said Cinderella.

'And actual blood!'

'Ruby red!' said Cinderella. 'Poor Buttons, but wasn't it worth it?'

'They make me sneeze, and he gives me the shivers,' said poor gloomy Buttons. 'Him and his roses. He laughed at my thumb.'

'Laughed?'

'Well, smiled. Bloodthirsty, I call it!'

'Poor Buttons,' said Cinderella, and to cheer him up she carefully unwound the bandage on his thumb and looked for the place where the thorn had been. It was not easy to see, even when Buttons stood in the sun and pointed to the exact agonizing spot.

'He's daft about those roses,' said Buttons. 'He loves them.'

'So would I,' said Cinderella.

'He's worst about the red ones.'

'Are there other colours?'

'They start off snow-white, but he doesn't like that. And some of them's blue . . .'

'Blue?'

'An 'orrible blue, like a bruise, but the Prince puts gloves on and weeds them out. Sighing and groaning.'

'Oh, the poor Prince!'

'Poor! The Prince!' scoffed Buttons, repacking his bag with polished boots. 'You'll see how poor he is on Friday!'

'How will I see on Friday?'

'At the palace ball!'

'There's to be a palace ball?'

For one long moment Cinderella's heart stopped beating.

'Everybody knows he has to find a wife – and that's how they find 'em, princes: at balls,' continued Buttons, not noticing Cinderella's suddenly pale cheeks. 'All the town's invited, but no princesses! That's the Prince's orders! "None of those blue-blood royals," he says.

'I've had all the invitations to give out. Here's yours!' Then, to Cinderella's utter amazement, Buttons reached into the boot sack and pulled out a large ruby-red envelope, scented with roses, and addressed to her in gold ink. And while Cinderella was still staring, he wound the bandage back around his thumb, picked up his sack, and hopped off over the wall.

'Buttons!' cried Cinderella. 'Buttons! Come back!'
Buttons' head popped back over the wall.
'I can't go, Buttons!'
'Why ever not?' asked Buttons, rather indignantly.
'I haven't got anything to wear!'

'That's what all the girls say,' said Buttons. 'Every single one I give an invitation to.'

'And then what happens?' asked Cinderella.

'They rush to the shops,' said Buttons simply.

'Oh,' said Cinderella. 'Oh well, never mind. Thank you for the lovely invitation. I'll keep it always. You do see that I can't rush to the shops, don't you, Buttons?'

Buttons looked at Cinderella, at her tatty slippers, her empty pockets, her brave eager smile and her wide blue eyes, and he said the wrong thing.

'There was one girl didn't rush to the shops . . .' he began.

'Was there? Was there? Oh, what will she wear?' asked Cinderella breathlessly.

'But she . . .'

'Oh, if there were two of us not in new clothes,' said Cinderella, 'it wouldn't matter so much!'

'Yes,' said Buttons, 'but she . . .'

'It wouldn't matter hardly at all!' said Cinderella, and now her eyes were sparkling, and her smile was radiant.

'Yes-but-she-remembered-her-yellow-silk-dress,' said Buttons, all in a rush.

'Yellow silk?' asked Cinderella in a very small voice.

'Yellow silk and green shoes and dangly green earrings. I think it'll look awful.'

Cinderella's brown head dropped, and when she looked up again the sparkle had gone from her eyes.

It was a minute before she could get her voice steady enough to whisper, 'I think it will look lovely.'

It was another minute more before she could say, 'Anyway, I don't care. It will probably be boring.'

And after that, there was nothing left to say, and Buttons had gone, back to the palace with his bag of polished boots.

◇

The first person he met back at the palace was the Prince, who was either talking to himself, or talking to his roses. Buttons had no respect for people who did either of those things, and so when he heard the Prince murmur, 'It will be much better after the ball!' he sprang into immediate rudeness.

'I don't see why,' he said. 'A boring ball won't change anything. What does that writing mean?'

The Prince, who had been holding a label fastened to the stem of a rose, turned it carefully over so that only the blank side was visible, and looked thoughtfully at Buttons, half questioning, half amused.

'Can you read?' he enquired, and he took out a gold pencil and wrote on the back of the label, *Buttons if you can read this, I will give you three silver pennies.*

'I can read that,' said Buttons. 'Only I don't want to.'

'Excellent,' said the Prince, smiling. 'The ball won't be boring.'

'My friend says it will.'

'What friend?'

'A girl.'

'She'll change her mind when she gets here,' said the Prince calmly.

'She's not coming!

'Everyone is coming,' said the Prince, still smiling.

'She's not. She told me. She's not got nothing to wear.'

'Hasn't got *anything* to wear,' corrected the Prince, pulling down a spray of roses. 'Smell a rose! Everyone is coming. Arrangements have been made for all circumstances. It won't be boring. Oh dear, did you prick your nose?'

'Not that you care!' said cross little Buttons.

'*Au contraire*, my poor damaged friend,' said the Prince, charmingly. 'I care very much indeed.'

◇

Cinderella's stepmother and stepsisters were completely thrilled about the ball. The sisters rushed to the shops and bought pink satin and green velvet and purple shoes and gold sandals and bangles and beads and bags to match. All these things appeared in the kitchen to be stitched and ironed and polished and strapped, and Cinderella's stepsisters appeared too, with requests concerning Sudden Diets, Tryings-On, and The Holding of Mirrors so they could see what they looked like from the back. There was a good deal of snapping and slapping at first, but as time went on, and the outfits became perfect, the stepsisters mellowed.

'How do we look?' they asked, as the evening of the ball finally arrived. And Cinderella replied most truthfully that they looked more beautiful than they had ever looked before. This put them in very good tempers, and they waltzed with each other round and round the kitchen, and Cinderella waltzed with the broom, and for that little space of time it was as if she was part of the magic.

But as suddenly as it had begun, it ended. The stepsisters gathered their beads and their dresses and fled away, and there was nothing left to show that they had been there, except a scattering of sequins and snippets of silk. Cinderella picked them up one by one until she held them all in her hand, a handful of brightness in the cold grey kitchen.

Then she sat at the table with her head in her arms and she said very quietly, 'Oh, I wish I could go to the ball.'

◇

She was still sitting there, when she heard the voices.

Buttons' voice, high and squeaky: 'She doesn't want to go! She told me!'

And another voice, very old and cross and deep: 'Move away from the door AT ONCE!'

At the word 'ONCE' there was a flash of bright light, the door flung itself inwards, and there was Buttons, spread like a starfish on the doormat, his eyes tight shut and his mouth wide open, and a very tall, very bony old woman stepping over him.

'I am here for the young person who owns no clothes,' this person announced to Cinderella. 'Kindly show me where I might find her.'

Cinderella, speechless with surprise, shook her head.

'She means you,' said Buttons, still with his eyes screwed shut.

'*Me?*' said Cinderella, a little outraged. '*Me?* I have clothes! I have this dress and my brown dress and my apron and two pairs of . . .'

'For the ball!' interrupted Buttons, now sitting up and glaring. 'You said you had nothing to wear for the ball and I told the Prince and the Prince told her . . .'

Buttons stopped speaking and blinked, rubbed his dazzled eyes and stared, first at Cinderella, then at the visitor, then back at Cinderella again. Silently, without the faintest murmur of a spell, or the quietest crackle of magic, she had been transformed.

'Why,' he demanded huskily, 'are you dressed like *that*?'

It sparkled like woven snowflakes, and whispered as Cinderella moved, and it was very soft and light. It was the most beautiful dress she had ever seen or imagined.

'Oh!' exclaimed Cinderella. 'But how . . . ?'

'Clearly you haven't read your invitation very

carefully,' snapped Buttons' strange companion. 'People always skip the small print. I suggest you look at it properly now.'

As if in a dream, Cinderella crossed the kitchen to the shadowy alcove where she slept, lifted the invitation from beneath her thin little pillow, and carried it into the light of the lamp.

'On the back!' directed the old woman.

'*Dress code*,' read Cinderella aloud, '*A S A P.*'

'As Sumptuous As Possible,' translated the old woman.

'*F G P.*'

'Fairy Godmothers Provided.'

'*S C R.*'

'Should Circumstances Require.'

'Then,' said Cinderella in delight, 'you are my fairy godmother!'

'*F L T O,*' said the old woman, pointing at the small print with a long finger. 'For Limited Time Only . . . until midnight, in fact. At midnight, that dress, those pearls in your hair . . .'

Cinderella's hands moved up in astonishment.

'. . . the necklace and bracelets . . .'

They were cool against her skin.

'. . . those enchanting glass slippers . . .'

'Glass slippers!' marvelled Cinderella, and began whirling round and round, shining with joy and pearls.

'Those four winged ponies attached to the golden coach at the door . . .'

It was true, they waited there.

'. . . will vanish!' said the fairy godmother sadly. 'Will all be gone. Do you understand, child?'

'I don't,' remarked Buttons.

'It's magic, isn't it?' whispered Cinderella. 'Thank you, thank you, thank you . . .'

She was touching the ponies' velvet muzzles, her snowflake dress was floating with the movement of their wings, she was in the coach and it was flying. Over the wall and over the rooftops and over the river, a golden light in a whirl of stars. She looked down to Buttons, still on the doormat.

'Run after her!' commanded the fairy godmother, prodding him to his feet. 'Run after her and say, "Midnight!" Make sure she understands.'

Buttons found himself gripped by his jacket, heaved high in the air by a long bony arm and dropped over the wall. He squeaked, stumbled, and ran.

◇

Ever since sunset, the palace had been shining with light. It sparkled with reflections from gilt cups and jewelled heels and crystal lamps. It hummed and throbbed and tinkled and murmured with voices and music and iced drinks and dance steps.

It smelt of roses.

At the top of the palace steps, under the brightest lamps of all, stood the Prince. To each guest that entered he handed a rose. He had a great tub of them, waiting.

'Welcome!' he said, his smile gallant, his eyes watchful. 'Be happy! Let me give you a rose!'

Then every guest, eager or shy, gabbling or silent, in silk or velvet or muslin or brocade, laughing or shivering, said, 'OUCH! It pricked me! I think it's bleeding!'

And each time the Prince was solemnly concerned and inspected the wound and recommended ice, but under his breath he murmured, 'Purple, purple, blue,

pink, blue, reddish, mauve, mauve, blue again (I SAID no princesses), pink, I suppose you might call that red . . .'

'Far too much blue!' he snapped at the Butler, during a lull in guests.

And the Butler, who was standing behind him with the ice, said, 'Very hard to weed them out, Sire. Very determined.'

The Prince groaned, turned to the next guest (who if she wasn't wearing a tiara, was wearing something very much like one) and selected her a nice spiky rose.

'OUCH!' she shrieked.

And the Prince peered and muttered, 'Just as I thought. Royal blue. Useless.'

But at last the crowd on the steps grew smaller. The roses in the tubs were almost all gone. 'Three, two, one, and that's the lot,' the Prince counted under his breath. 'Purple, mauve, wishy-washy pink . . . Look at that! I don't believe it!'

A little gold coach was flying up the drive.

'That's a princess if ever I saw one!' said the Prince angrily to the Butler. 'Take over, will you? I can't be bothered.'

But before this could happen, Cinderella jumped from her coach and, despite himself, the Prince paused.

'Oh how lovely, lovely, lovely!' cried Cinderella, running up the steps. 'Oh, Buttons never told me it was as beautiful as *this*! Oh, thank you for asking me! Oh, is that for me?'

It was the last rose in the tub, rather squashed and damp, a white one, not even red, but it was Cinderella's first rose, and she loved it, smelt it, touched the petals to her cheek, laughed out loud in delight, and tucked it into the front of her dress.

'It's only a white one,' said the Prince, watching.

'It has a golden heart,' said Cinderella. 'It's absolutely perfect. I like the white ones best.'

'Did it prick you?' asked the Prince.

'No,' Cinderella shook her head and bent to smile at her rose. 'Anyway, if it had, it would have been worth it. Oh, I recognize your boots!'

The Prince, despite very much mistrusting her snowflake dress and the golden carriage, looked at Cinderella with more interest than he had looked at anyone for hours, and raised his first eyebrow of the evening.

'I polished them last Tuesday,' explained Cinderella helpfully. 'I help Buttons. He's a friend. Listen to that music! Can we go inside?'

The Prince bowed to his boots and held out a hand, and the first thing Cinderella said when she saw the glistening ballroom was, 'However do you keep it clean?'

'I believe there are . . . um . . . servants,' said the

Prince, after thinking for a moment, 'and er . . . possibly brooms.'

'I have a broom,' Cinderella told him. 'A very good broom. I dance with it . . .' (The Prince's eyebrows were getting no rest now, shooting up and down at almost every new thing Cinderella said.) 'I dance and sweep the kitchen at the same time. They say it wears out the bristles, but I think it's worth it.'

By now she and the Prince were dancing, the shiny boots and the sparkling glass slippers waltzing in perfect time. 'It's much, *much* better with a real person,' Cinderella gasped, laughing. 'My darling broom doesn't spin like this at all. We do quite slow twirls, compared . . . Oh, there's Buttons!'

Buttons saw Cinderella at the same time, shot across the dance floor, grabbed her skirts, and squeaked, 'Midnight! Don't forget!'

'What happens at midnight?' asked the Prince.

'Oh,' said Cinderella, suddenly mournful. 'Let's not think about that. It's ages, isn't it, till midnight?'

'Perhaps,' said the Prince. 'Shall we dance again? And you can tell me how you came to meet Buttons.'

The stories that followed, of washtubs and bubbles and muddy stockings arriving by pulleys to be scrubbed in the kitchen, of sparrows on doorsteps and cobwebs and shadows and coal and log buckets and the Prince's own boots, gave the Prince's eyebrows more exercise than they had ever had before . . . and meanwhile the dancers whirled, and the lamps shone, and voices laughed, and the roses round the palace walls poured their perfume through the open windows.

'Would you mind,' Cinderella asked at last, 'if we stopped dancing for a little while to give my rose a drink?'

The Prince nodded, and his eyebrows became very thoughtful as he watched Cinderella untuck her little white rose and lower it gently into a glass of cool champagne. 'I should like it to last forever,' Cinderella explained, smiling up at him. 'The golden middle . . .'

'Stamens . . .' the Prince told her.

'. . . the stamens glow so brightly, like a little sun! And the petals are as white as moonlight.'

'The petals are heart-shaped,' said the Prince, so suddenly that Cinderella jumped.

'Yes,' she whispered.

'Although I prefer the ruby-red,' said the Prince, very briskly. 'Here comes your little friend again!'

'Midnight!' panted Buttons, clutching Cinderella to steady himself as he skidded across the floor.

'Not yet, not yet,' said Cinderella. 'Buttons, look at my rose!'

'They make me sneeze,' said Buttons. 'There are too many blooming roses around here!'

'There can never be too many blooming roses,

Buttons,' said Cinderella, laughing.

'You're as bad as him,' said Buttons, frowning at the Prince. 'You've been dancing together an awful lot. Everyone's saying it's time he danced with someone else.'

The Prince glared at Buttons, and then his eyes shot round the ballroom. The sudden waiting silence that fell confirmed that Buttons was speaking the truth.

'What about the one in the red dress?' asked Buttons.

'Half of them at least are wearing red dresses,' said the Prince irritably.

'That's because you're always hanging over them red roses,' said Buttons. 'They think you'll notice them more. What about her that's waving that big fan? She asked me special to make you look at her.'

'Oh ALL right!' snapped the Prince. 'Stop pointing! I'm going. Stay where you are, I'll be back.'

But Cinderella didn't wait for the Prince to come back because she couldn't bear to waste the time. 'Come on!' she said to Buttons.

'I'm not dancing with girls,' said Buttons in disgust. 'I can't anyway, I don't know how, I don't like it, everyone will laugh.'

'Pretend you're a broom, and I'll dance you,' said Cinderella. 'That's right! That's perfect! Round the kitchen, sweep, sweep! Mind the table, spin! Try not to clump in case they hear upstairs! Brilliant, Buttons!'

Buttons smirked, and when the Prince came back and

tapped him on his head, he dashed off to find another girl with whom to sweep the floor.

'I do love Buttons,' said Cinderella to the Prince.

'He's much too young for you,' said the Prince briskly. 'Are glass slippers comfortable?'

'Not at all,' said Cinderella, 'but so pretty they are worth it.'

'Would you like to stop dancing and rest for a while?'

'I'd like to dance forever,' said Cinderella.

But time was passing, and Buttons was much too occupied now to remember to look at the clock. There was supper and fireworks and a trip up to the highest turret to look down on the roses from above, and then everyone was back in the ballroom again and it was half past eleven and then a quarter to twelve and then later and later and later and at one minute to twelve o' clock Buttons suddenly remembered, dropped his latest partner and shrieked, 'Midnight!'

And then Cinderella remembered too.

Cinderella left the Prince, rescued her rose, and fled across the ballroom and out into the cool night air of the palace steps. The little gold coach waited at the foot, the wings of the four white ponies beating with impatience.

'Wait! Wait!' cried Cinderella, but the steps were slippery with faded petals and melted ice cubes, and the glass slippers were losing their magic. Halfway down, Cinderella fell.

It hurt very much. One slipper broke and cut her foot. The other was lost in the darkness. The pearls in her hair rolled away down the steps, her snowflake dress melted into her shabby grey frock, and the little gilt coach with the four winged ponies rose into the sky without her. Cinderella gazed as it faded . . .

a golden blur . . .

the furthest star . . .

gone.

Then Cinderella picked herself up and limped down the palace steps, across the bridge and the deserted market-place, over the wall, and back to the kitchen, where the fire was out and the shadows were deep, and she curled up in her little cold bed.

But the last thing she thought, before she went to sleep, was, *It was worth it*.

◊

Back at the palace, the ball went on. The music, and

the lamplight, and the dancing. Buttons was soon back on the ballroom floor again, having discovered that dancing with girls was the thing he liked best. He forgot Cinderella as soon as she vanished.

But the Prince did not. He went looking. All through the palace, around by the roses, at the top of the highest turret, and then, one by one, he searched the white marble steps. Just as the sun rose, he saw the glass slipper.

He saw something else too, and it made his heart beat hard and fast.

Then the Prince went leaping back up to the palace.

◇

The last and best thing about a really good ball is the magnificent breakfast served early in the morning before the dancers go home. This was what was happening when the Prince ran back into the palace ballroom.

'Buttons will know where she is! Buttons! Where is that dismal child, Buttons?' shouted the Prince, rushing between the boiled eggs and fresh peaches and buttered toast and muffins and pancakes and waffles and ham and honey and raspberries and porridge and kippers being consumed by his guests.

They bowed and curtsied, shook their heads and shrugged their shoulders, gulped and swallowed and said, 'He was here a minute ago.'

But Buttons, who had eaten a French loaf, a side of

smoked salmon, six eggs and one hundred and twenty-two strawberries, had fallen asleep on a window seat, tucked up in a heap of borrowed velvet cloaks. He was quite invisible and quite deaf to the world, and he stayed that way for several hours while the Prince, in his frantic searching, ran past him many times. Meanwhile the guests went home, and the (by now exhausted) Butler was sent out to the marketplace with a Royal Proclamation (which is a loud, forceful message written on a long scroll in very black ink).

The Royal Proclamation said that whoever fitted the glass slipper, carried by the Palace Butler on a purple velvet cushion, was sought by the Prince most urgently.

'She must be the one he's chosen to marry!' exclaimed many voices in the crowd.

The girl in the red dress who had flapped the very large fan said, 'What if she doesn't want to?' But she was the only one. The entire guest list, including Cinderella's stepsisters, queued up in the marketplace to try on the slipper, and it didn't fit any of them.

'That's because it's Cinderella's,' said Buttons, staggering amongst them, awake at last.

Then urgent messages were sent to the palace for the Prince to come at once, while Buttons said importantly, 'Follow me!' and led the Butler round to the back of Cinderella's house and over the wall, and across the yard and into the shadowy kitchen.

And, astonishing! There was Cinderella, with her arms round the neck of a stranger, who, with his cheek resting gently on her brown silk hair, was murmuring, 'My dear. My dearest.'

It didn't seem the moment for proclamations and shoe fittings, and the Butler realized this and frogmarched Buttons outside again. They stood guard at the door together. The worn-out Butler soon fell asleep (standing up, like horses do), but Buttons passed the time reading the Royal Proclamation. That is what he was doing when the Prince climbed over the wall with his arms full of roses.

'Oh, it's you,' said Buttons. 'You can't go in. She's busy.'

'But is she safe? Is she happy? Is she *all right*?' demanded the Prince.

'She is now,' said Buttons. 'But where's her other shoe?'

'Smashed,' said the Prince, and once again felt the lurch of his heart at the memory of the broken crystal and the small red marks on the white marble steps.

'One shoe's no good,' said Buttons, and went back to his reading, and this time the Prince noticed.

And stared.

'You can read!' he said.

'Three silver pennies!' said Buttons triumphantly, holding out his hand. 'I can read. I read that label. I told you I did! I read it on both sides! "*Rosa alba. White roses. Can be grown as Rosa rubens vampira in certain conditions.*" Bloodthirsty roses! And royal blood turns them a very nasty blue!'

'Yes, it does,' admitted the Prince. 'But un-royal blood, commoners' blood, like yours . . .'

'Oi!' growled Buttons, insulted.

'Proper, priceless, perfectly-normal-people's blood,' said the Prince, appeasingly polite, 'turns them beautiful ruby red, and it only takes a drop. And that's why I didn't want any blue-blooded princesses at my ball.'

'In case you married one by mistake and she went and ruined your roses?' said Buttons.

'Exactly,' said the Prince.

But although he had given the palace ball for the sake of his ruby-red roses as much as the need for a wife, he had fallen in love with Cinderella hours before he had seen her footprint on the marble steps. And by then he didn't care if she was royal or not, if only she loved him back. And the roses he had brought her were all white with golden stamens, because that was the colour she said she loved most.

And their petals were heart-shaped.

And he had taken off every thorn.

So the Prince went into the house and found Cinderella.

And Cinderella said, 'Darling Daddy, this is the

Prince. Darling Prince, this is Daddy.'

And such happiness filled the kitchen that all the shadows vanished.

◇

Then, not long afterwards, Cinderella married the Prince and went to live at the palace, and she and the Prince took care of the roses together, and they took care of Cinderella's father and of Buttons too. Later they had two round baby boys to take care of as well, and then two round baby girls. And with Cinderella at the palace, there was much bubble-blowing and dancing and many sparrows on the marble steps and everybody, always, polished their own boots.

And the roses around the palace walls were white with golden hearts, except sometimes, when Cinderella pricked her fingers on purpose and turned them ruby red.

'I don't think you ought to do that,' said Buttons, prim and shuddering, but Cinderella laughed at him from amongst the perfume-pouring flowers.

'Dear, dear Buttons!' she said. 'It truly doesn't hurt. And anyway . . .

'*I* think it's worth it!'

4

The Fountain in the Market Square

or
The Pied Piper of Hamelin

Patter, patter, patter

Silver rain

That

is

The fountain in the market square

and I am the Mayor of Hamelin.

The fountain was given to the city by my great-grandfather more than one hundred years ago. The date is carved on the steps beneath:

1185
A Gift to the Good People of Hamelin

Hamelin, my little city. A pleasant city, with its church bells and market bustle, its red roofs and white walls, and its garland of green hills beyond the river.

I admit, one year the rats were a problem.

Why were there so many rats that year? Some people blame the river. Others remember the good harvest of the autumn before, the grain stores full to bursting, the cheeses and the butter tubs. The dried fruits and the wines and the stores of meadow honeycomb. But I am not so sure. The river always ran beside the city. We have been fortunate: there have often been good harvests. No one went hungry in Hamelin. Not the hardworking merchants, nor the busy housewives, nor the old folk in their rocking chairs, not the merry young people in the streets.

When I was young, things were different. Perhaps not better, but different. This city of ours did not fall from the sky like a toy ready-made, its streets swept, its merchants stocked, its bread baked, the window-boxes full of herbs, and the chimneys ready smoking!

Not at all! Hard work made our city. Hard work from all, even the young. The boys learned their fathers' trades: up early in the morning, and steady at it until the candles burned out at night. The girls were little housewives as soon as they could walk. They swept and baked and made and mended, dried their herbs and pounded spices. They kept their hair hidden in snow-white caps, and in church they held their eyes modestly down.

Oh, they were good girls! Good girls and boys! I remember Sunday services! The boys in their best jackets. The glimpse of a girl's curved cheek under a bonnet enough to keep you dreaming for a week!

Not like the young people of Hamelin that came afterwards! Why, they could hardly be hauled inside a church. The boys whistling in the streets with their hands in their pockets. The girls! There were no more white caps hiding their hair! Curls and braids, ribbons too, if they could get them, scarlet and blue and gold. And the boys just as bad, with bright feathers in their hats.

I never wore a feather in my life, when I was a boy. Nor would they, if they had had my father. And after all, what harm is a feather? Or a ribbon? I expect my sister would have liked a ribbon. Perhaps. Perhaps not. I cannot guess; I hardly knew her. Boys and girls kept separate in those days.

◇

There was no keeping separate for the next generation. No. They gathered round the steps of the fountain with apples from the market and rolls from the bakers, sausage from the butcher, cheese from the dairy. Dropping crumbs. A picnic in the market square. Never ever in my day.

It would be unkind at this time to say that the young people brought the rats to Hamelin, and I do not say it.

However, the rats came. Undoubtedly the river was the cause. Or the good harvest.

At first we only heard the creatures at night. A scratching under the floorboards and spoilt bread in the morning. Then we would catch glimpses by daylight, timid, racing along under the shadow of a wall.

Although already you could smell them.

When the warm weather of spring arrived, the numbers doubled, tripled, became ten times as many, almost overnight.

And the noise they made! Before, the night noises in the street had been the games of the young people. Now it was the squeals and scrabbles of rats. Huge rats. Fighting rats. Unafraid, daylight rats. Rats that leaped from cupboards and crawled over pillows and fought such battles in the house walls that you could see the plaster bulge. Rats amongst the rafters, and rats sliding from the drains. Fat rats crawling up from the graveyard in the morning. The whole city paying the price of those picnics around my grandfather's fountain.

Although it may well have been the nearness of the river.

Or the harvest.

Of course.

In late spring then, in the worst of it, came the Piper.

The Pied Piper, the young people called him (they had names for everyone). Pied he was however, many-coloured, bright and dark. Cloak and jacket and breeches, all stripes and bands of red and white and blue and gold and green. High-stepping red leather boots, and a long shining pipe, a valuable thing. Silver overlaid with gold, I would say. I know about such matters.

The first I knew of the Piper arriving was his hammering at the door of the city hall.

'I heard you had a problem,' he said, the corners of his mouth curled up in a smile (as a rat ran over my feet). 'Perhaps I can help you,' said he.

Bright blue eyes flashing sparks like sunlight on water. I didn't take to him.

'A slight inconvenience,' I said. 'The natural result of our closeness to the river . . .' (a rat fell out of my pocket) '. . . or perhaps the excellent harvest . . .' (three more tumbled squeaking down the steps) '. . . or possibly . . .' I added, frowning at two graceless young lads grinning across at me from the fountain steps '. . . the careless behaviour of the young. Whatever, the situation is completely under control.'

A rat, as large as a small dog, sat squarely down by my foot and began to comb its whiskers. When I pushed it away, it sank its long yellow teeth into the lacings of my boots and would not be shaken free.

'Completely under control,' repeated the Piper. (Did he wink at the boys? I think he did.) 'Excellent! Then you have no need of a poor rat-catcher such as me.'

That was the first I knew of him being a rat-catcher, and he had already turned away.

'Stay! Wait!' I cried, as he went striding across the market square. 'My good fellow! Stay!'

'Good fellow?' he asked, and nodded as if pleased.

'Should I, should the city, have need of a rat-catcher,' I panted (ignoring the smirks of those boys), 'what would be . . . How much should we . . . What would you charge?'

'For how many rats?' he enquired, briskly.

'For all the rats in Hamelin,' I said (glaring across at the fountain steps, where quite a crowd had collected).

The Piper raised an eyebrow as he looked down at me (he was tall). 'For all the rats in Hamelin,' he said. 'Well. For every ten, a guilder!'

'What?' I cried. 'Impossible!' For a guilder is a good sum of money in Hamelin. You might buy a large loaf of bread for a guilder, or a tankard of brown ale. 'A guilder for each ten?' I said. 'There must be a thousand rats in the city!'

'Ten thousand,' said the Piper.

'That would mean a thousand guilders!' I exclaimed,

calculating rapidly. 'My dear fellow, this city cannot afford a thousand guilders!'

'Then goodbye,' said the Piper cheerfully, 'so long as this city can afford ten thousand rats!'

And he stepped away in his long red boots as merrily as if he were going off to a wedding, while I, tripping and stumbling, pushed through the crowd at the fountain (if I had sons and daughters, which I am quite resigned to say I do not, I hope they would not laugh out loud at the sight of a gentleman, an elderly gentleman, hurrying to do his best for the city). And with that blasted creature from the city hall steps still clinging to my boot, I ran after him, and I caught him up at last . . . and when I had got my breath, I panted, 'I agree!'

'To what do you agree?' asked the Piper. 'A guilder for every ten rats dead?'

'A guilder for every ten dead rats,' I said, and held out my hand.

'And for ten thousand rats?' asked the Piper.

'A thousand guilders,' I replied.

Then the Piper shook my hand.

◇

The work of the Piper that day was a wonder to see. He ordered the streets cleared, and all the people behind doors, though we might watch from the windows, he said. And then he stood by the fountain in the market square, where I believe all the trouble had started, and he raised his pipe and played.

I do not care for music. I never did. But that is one tune that I would listen to again.

Clear and sweet, like a blackbird's song. Lilting, like a dance. Merry, then wistful, then merry again.

And the rats!

I had guessed a thousand. The Piper said ten. I think there were more. There were rats beyond counting. They poured from doorways, rose from drains, leaped from windows, and they raced and pushed after the Piper, like puppies greeting a friend. He needed his high-stepping boots: at times he was knee-deep. He walked past the church, and they fell on to his shoulders from the steeple. They fought and struggled to greet him. They became not one rat, and then another, but a crawling, heaving single mass. If the Piper had fallen, I believe he would have been engulfed, but he did not. Slowly, slowly, always piping, he led them through the city streets. They rustled and scrabbled after him, and with them, like a cloud, went the musty, sickly, throat-catching stench of rat.

I never want to smell such a smell again, so thick in the air that you could taste it.

For hours the Piper piped. It was nearly sundown before he reached the river gate. He passed through, and led the rats down to the crossing place, down to the ford, and that was their fate and the end of them.

The river was running fast that day, and every rat that had tormented this city was swept away. Swept away and drowned.

Every one.

Gone.

◇

A thousand guilders is a great deal of money. True, there were tens of thousands in the city's treasure house, but to spend so much on one day's work?

A thousand guilders of the city's hard-earned wealth for the work of one man, on one day?

A guilder for every ten dead rats, and we had shaken hands.

◇

At nightfall the Piper came back to the city hall. He looked a different man. He looked aged. He looked ill.

Staggering.

White-faced, exhausted. Soaked from the river and filthy.

There were no blue sparks left in his eyes, and though his hand still held his pipe, it trembled.

'You had a hard day's work,' I said kindly to him.

'I had,' said he. 'The hardest I ever had, but the job's done.'

'Done and well done,' I agreed. 'Excellent!'

'A thousand guilders,' said he.

'Indeed, indeed.' I smiled. (I was the smiler this

time, not he. And I had been thinking.) 'I remember the bargain. We shook hands, my friend. A guilder for every ten dead rats!'

He nodded.

'So where are the dead rats then, my man?'

'Eh?' he asked, shaking his head.

'I see no rats,' I explained. 'No dead rats.'

He rubbed his sleeve across his eyes as if to clear his vision, and he looked dumbly at me.

'I have to think of the city,' I explained, gently, as if to a child. 'A thousand guilders of the city's money, and no proof that the job is done. No dead rats. No proof.'

'No proof?' he said slowly.

'And so no reason,' I continued briskly, 'to spend such a sum as a thousand guilders on one day's work. But in thanks for your help . . .'

'Help,' he said. (He kept repeating my words. But then, he was tired. Bone weary, I could see that. So I held my patience.)

'. . . in thanks for your great help, a purse is ready. Fifty guilders!'

And I held it out. Fifty bright guilders in a fine leather bag.

'An excellent day's pay!' I said, speaking heartily to cheer him. 'Not another fellow in Hamelin earns so much in a day! And there is a free night's lodging waiting at the inn for you, with a good supper too.

The best room. I arranged it myself.'

'You are cheating me?' he asked.

'My dear . . .' I began.

'After such a day! After such a deed! Fifty guilders!'

'Take it or leave it,' I said. (I was annoyed, I admit. I had filled the purse. I had arranged the inn. I had thanked him heartily. I had explained.)

'Take it or leave it!' he exploded. 'After such a day, you owe me a thousand guilders! I'll either take what you can spare, or I'll take what you cannot spare! What's it to be?'

'Take the purse!' I ordered. But he turned his back and walked away through the city streets, and I never saw him again.

◇

Well. Of course I was worried. 'I'll take what you can spare, or I'll take what you cannot spare!' I remembered those words. I made sure to lock up my silver plates that night, and my gold chain and the emerald ring I had from my grandfather. I locked, and double-locked the chests, and then I went out into the city streets.

The streets were clear of rats, free of rats. The city was released.

◇

The next day we all rejoiced! The men stopped up rat holes. The women scrubbed and swept. And everywhere I went I was thanked and praised and clapped on the back, and applauded for a hero. The streets seem to glow with colour that day, and the sky was very blue, and the wind blew clean from the hills. 'Oh,' I heard a young lad exclaim to a girl. (He was sweeping, all right, I admit, he was helping with the work.) 'Oh Rosa, we shall have our picnics again!'

Great heavens, the foolishness of the young! I turned to speak my mind, but he had dropped his brush and scampered away.

By Sunday the city was clean, and we went to church to give thanks.

For we were truly thankful.

Every pew was filled that morning, and every aisle packed, and no room for the youngsters, even if they had wanted. But as I have said before, the young people of Hamelin preferred the streets as a rule. I doubt many of them were sorry they could not get into church that day.

Not then.

Not at the time.

Well, I sat there in church and I counted my blessings. The rats gone. The money saved. My silver plates and gold chain and emerald ring all safely locked away. The praise I had had for my cleverness, and the thanks of the people of the city. I tried not to think of the silly young sweeping lad, or the girl, Rosa (whoever she was). But I could not help thinking of the Piper, dead weary at the end of the day. I wished he had taken the fifty guilders and rested the night at the inn.

Well, he was a fool to refuse! Him and his pipe! Nothing but a rat-catcher; what more did he expect? People expect too much these days! Look at the youngsters! Listen to the youngsters!

My seat was by the entrance, and it being such a hot day, and the church so full, the door had been left a little way open. I could hear the youngsters on the street, chattering like birds.

I never knew such a long service. There were readings and prayers and a sermon that seemed endless.

Perhaps I dozed.

Perhaps I dozed, and it was only in a dream that I heard the Piper again.

I heard sweet, calling notes, dropped one by one, like silver guilders, and then a lilting melody.

I know my eyes were closed. I kept them closed. No one else seemed to hear.

As the music came closer, the bird chatter grew brighter, then ceased, and then began again.

All the time the melody, and all the time the Piper passing, and the chatter fading, fading with the patter, patter of footsteps.

The rustle of girls' skirts, and the clatter of the wooden clogs that the poorest boys used to wear.

That was all.

And what if I'd done things differently?

What if I'd opened my eyes?

What if I'd raced to the door and flung it open and cried out, 'Stop! Come back!'

What if I'd rushed into the street and seized the Piper, torn his pipe from his lips?

What if I'd pleaded, 'Forgive me! Friend, forgive me!' Hurried him to the city treasure house! Dragged out the chests! Heaped gold and silver at his feet!

What if I'd begged, on my knees?

What then?

Would that have been right?

Would that have been responsible?

Would that have been dignified?

No.

So there I sat, and the service ended, and the church emptied, and still I sat.

Thinking.

I thought two things:

1. There were no witnesses to what was said between myself and the Piper, when he refused so unreasonably to take his fee.
2. Is it so wrong that a tired man should close his eyes in church?

◇

There were three left behind. A sick boy who lay in bed with fever and knew nothing of the matter. The little deaf girl from the candlemaker's house. She understood too late that her fellows were leaving the city. No matter, she is a good quiet girl.

The last was a lame boy, and it was he who told the story, blubbering with tears at the end of the day. This is what he told:

He had spotted the Piper from afar, his bright colours in the market square. He had seen him glance round at the young people gathered there, nod, and lift his pipe. He had heard those first sweet, calling notes, and at once begun to hurry, and he caught up with the crowd as the melody began.

It was like a dance, he said, that started slow and

grew quicker and quicker. Through the city and out into the countryside, and all the time, faster and faster, the Piper played, with his crowd hurrying after him, running to keep up, and although the lame boy begged them, 'Wait!' they did not seem to hear.

He was left far behind, but still he heard the music, floating backwards on the wind, and still he followed.

'Until it was too late,' he said, sniffing and dripping and wiping his nose on his sleeve, 'and they were gone.'

'Where? Gone where?' demanded the desperate fathers and mothers of Hamelin, and he told them, 'Into the great hill. I saw them go into the great hill. A doorway opened and closed for them, and I was left outside.'

Now that is nonsense! A doorway in a hillside! But the boy was never bright. His brains were as slow as his legs. He was no help to the searchers that went out that night, and for many days and nights. And for weeks, and months. Until the cold weather closed down on the land, and they lost hope.

One hundred and thirty young people.

I never lost hope. I trust they are well. I am sure they are. Why would they not be?

And grief passes.

◇

Much good had come of the visit from the Piper.

The streets of our lovely city are clean and ordered. The nights are quiet again. No more noisy gatherings at the fountain, for instance!

Bringing rats. (Although it may have been the river, or the harvest.)

And babies are born.

And years pass, and we have a new generation of children.

How I like these new children! How I admire them! They are quiet and sober. The boys keep close to their fathers, learning to work. The girls stay safely indoors with their mothers. In the streets they are modest and timid. The boys do not whistle. Boys and girls both come to church without question.

In the market square the water of the fountain falls, and some say it weeps for the lost children.

Not me.

There is no need to think of weeping, not for me. Everything that I have done, or left undone, was for the sake of the city alone. Hamelin, my little city, with its church bells and red roofs and white walls, in the garland of green hills.

Patter, patter, patter
Silver rain
That
is
The fountain in the market square
and I am the Mayor of Hamelin.

5

Chickenpox and Crystal
or
Snow White and the Seven Dwarves

'Do I look all right?' asked Sophie. And then, because they both hesitated for one moment, less than a second, before replying, she said, 'You don't have to pretend! I know what you're thinking!'

Sophie's mother and grandmother both blinked, because this crossness was so unlike Sophie, and before their blinks were over, Sophie had flounced out of the door and stomped off along the corridor. The stomping went on for quite a while. That was one of the many problems of living in a large palace: it took so long between the flounce and the slamming of the bedroom door.

And of course the slam was a good way off from the flouncing point, and so might have been any old bang.

Sophie's mother hurried after her daughter. She was an understanding person. She knew herself what it felt like to be the only princess at a birthday party when you didn't know what everyone else would be wearing. She arrived at the slammed bedroom door, knocked on it and called, 'It's me!'

'Go away. I don't care. I know I look stupid, and I'm not going! Besides, I think I'm ill!' said Sophie.

Sophie's mother picked the easiest of these remarks to reply to and asked, 'What sort of ill?'

There was a thinking pause on the other side of the door, and then Sophie replied, 'Chickenpox.'

'Oh.'

'Like the cook had.'

'That was last year.'

'I don't care WHEN it was!' shouted Sophie through the door. 'I'm just NOT going to the party. I only got asked because they know you, and anyway my dress is all ripped.'

'It wasn't all ripped two minutes ago,' said her mother.

'That was before it got caught on the roses.'

'What roses?'

'The yellow ones outside my window.'

'Sophie!' exclaimed her mother. And she marched in, rescued the thrown-out-of-the-window dress, groaned, took an old one from the wardrobe, pulled it on over Sophie's head, fastened the back, brushed her hair, bundled her out of the room, along the corridor, down the stairs, across the hall, through the front door, over the terrace and into the waiting coach.

'Daddy and I won't be here when you get back, but you're having supper with your grandmother,' Sophie's mother said as she bundled her daughter inside. 'She's coming to visit especially to keep you company. Have a lovely time! The birthday present is on the seat beside you. It's a golden ball. I hope your friend likes it.'

'Nobody plays with golden balls any more!' protested Sophie, but the carriage was already driving away.

◇

Nothing had improved when Sophie returned from the party. She told her grandmother how she had accidentally taken a raw-fish sandwich and had to keep it in her pocket all afternoon because there was nowhere to throw it away. And how a girl had said, 'I didn't think a princess would look like you,' and one of the boys had added, 'Or smell like you!' And then everyone had sniffed, and said, 'Fishy!'

And the golden ball had been lost in the pond, and her shoes were soaked from trying to get it out, and she still thought she had chickenpox.

'Worse than ever!' said Sophie.

Later her parents came back, and then everyone considered Sophie, and they all agreed the same things:

Bed was the best place for her.
1. Of course she didn't have chickenpox.
2. This really wasn't like Sophie.

They didn't know that Sophie had a secret.

Sophie's secret was a fragment of glass, the size of an almond. It was very slightly cloudy, and silvered on the back. The broken edges were razor sharp: it was a breathless job to pick it up, but still Sophie treasured it. She thought that it was beautiful and she had discovered that it was magic.

Sophie had found that if she held it long enough, in her fingers and in her thoughts, the fragment had a voice.

A thin gnat's voice.

'*You,*' Sophie heard. '*You. You. You.*'

'Me?' wondered Sophie. 'Me!'

Sophie began to think thoughts that she had never had before: 'Who am I? What am I?' and most of all, 'Do you think I am pretty?'

'Yes, of course,' said Sophie's parents. But they had to say that because they were her father and mother.

'Yes,' said Sophie's grandmother. (But of course she had to say it too.) 'Do you?'

I want to be, thought this new Sophie. More than anything, I want to be pretty.

The glass fragment helped with that.

It was a strange thing, but if Sophie looked at herself in the bathroom mirror, or in the little round glass in her bedroom, or even in the curly-edged gold full-length mirror in her mother's room, then she saw ordinary Sophie. Straight brown hair, a round face, a few freckles, nice eyebrows like two painted brush strokes. Starfish hands and sturdy knees, tallish more than shortish.

But the glimpses of herself that she caught in the knife-edged fragment of ancient glass showed an altogether more beautiful person. So Sophie would find a glimmering strand of hair, a moment of flower-petal skin, a shadow of a dimple, a curl of a gold-tipped eyelash. Tiny fragments of herself, like one piece of a very large jigsaw. And also, if she waited long enough, she would hear in confirmation, '*You. You. You.*'

'Me?' wondered Sophie. 'Am I pretty? Am I? Am I the prettiest? Am I the prettiest one of all?'

'Sophie,' said Sophie's grandmother, 'what did you just ask?'

It was bedtime on the party day, and her grandmother had come to say goodnight.

'Am I the prettiest one of all?' repeated Sophie.

Sophie's grandmother was the best grandmother anyone could wish for. She was gentle and funny and clever and kind. She was pretty too, in an ancient way, with deep sparkling eyes and wrinkled pink cheeks. She loved Sophie so much that she could only ever tell her the truth.

'You are our best girl in the world,' she told Sophie. 'But no one is the prettiest! You can't have the prettiest cloud, or the prettiest buttercup, can you? And in the same way, you can't have the prettiest person. What are you holding in your hand?'

Sophie, who knew quite well that neither she nor anyone else should hold razor-sharp broken glass in their hand, pushed it under her pillow and said, 'Nothing.'

◇

'Sophie,' said Sophie's grandmother, downstairs in the palace drawing room, 'is not herself at all.'

And then morning came, and there was Sophie, dotted all over with little red spots.

'THAT'S what was wrong!' her family said. 'And we paid no attention! Poor Sophie! She was right all along!'

'Chickenpox,' they told Sophie, loving and sorry.

And Sophie said, 'I told you so.'

A palace, where your parents are king and queen, and there are people in and out all day, and everyone is busy and on best behaviour all the time, is no place to have chickenpox. And so Sophie was taken back to her grandmother's house, which was ten times smaller and a hundred times more comfortable. She took with her, wrapped in a handkerchief and held tight in her hand, the little piece of crystal. It cut through the handkerchief before she was halfway there, and she arrived with a bleeding palm, but even so, it was a great comfort to Sophie. She got it out as soon as she could, and it didn't show a single chickenpox spot.

And although Sophie could see very clearly the spots on her arms and legs and stomach, she couldn't see her face, and so she believed her glass fragment and didn't imagine them. This was especially easy at her grandmother's house, because there were hardly any mirrors there. Just a very small hand mirror in her grandmother's room, so, she said, she could check that her face was clean. Usually it lay face down on the dressing table.

'I don't care for mirrors,' said Sophie's grandmother.

The first chickenpox day was not nice. Sophie felt achy and hot and awful and thirsty and itchy and grumpy and miserable.

'My poor Sophie,' said her grandmother, and put her to bed with meadowsweet tea for the fever, and cool dabs of lotion, and tiny, delicious snacks of fruit and jelly, bread and butter in thin soft triangles, and iced lemon sponge fingers on a yellow plate. When evening came she opened the window so the breeze blew in and fluttered the curtains, and she said, 'Try and sleep,

Sophie. You'll feel better in the morning.'

Sophie did sleep, in hot and itchy bits and pieces, with her grandmother in and out with drinks and more dabs of lotion. Towards morning she slept properly, and woke up at dawn to find her grandmother fast asleep in the big chair by the window. She took her chance then, and scooped under her pillow for the almond-shaped piece of glass, and she smiled at what it showed her. It was just the same as the day before. Fragments of a very pretty person, and the same thin voice whispering, '*You, you, you!*'

Words came then to Sophie, and she spoke them aloud:

'Crystal treasure in my hand
Who is the prettiest in the land?'

'Sophie!' exclaimed her grandmother, waking with a jump, and she hurried across to Sophie with her kind, merry face looking suddenly frightened.

What had she heard? Sophie didn't know.

What had she seen? Sophie couldn't guess.

'Your hand is scratched,' said her grandmother. 'How did you cut it, Sophie?'

'It doesn't matter. It hardly hurts,' said Sophie.

Her grandmother looked at her, and Sophie looked away.

All the same, the scratch was washed, the chickenpox was bathed and dabbed, and Sophie's bed remade with clean, cool sheets. And after breakfast her grandmother brought in the old-fashioned toys that belonged in that house. Sophie had always loved them. Storybooks, and beads to thread, and spillikins, and a set of little wooden bears with comical faces and jointed legs. But their charm was gone with the chickenpox, and Sophie pushed them away one by one because they were too hard to bother with. Tears came to her eyes because she couldn't love them.

'They will still be here when you feel better,' said her grandmother when Sophie tried to explain. 'Would you like to go to sleep again?'

'No, no!' said Sophie.

'Then would you like the music box that plays a hundred tunes?'

'I'd hate it,' moaned Sophie.

'Shall I read to you?'

'I know all the stories in those books.'

'Then I will tell you a new one,' said her grandmother. 'A new true story from a long time ago, and the minute you have had enough you can tell me, and I'll save the rest for later.'

She began at once.

'Long ago, and far away, it was wintertime and snowing outside the palace windows. And by one of those windows, a young queen sat sewing, and she had the window open because she loved the tingle and sparkle of the falling snowflakes so much, and the sound they make . . . you know that sound, Sophie, like faraway bees.'

Sophie nodded.

'Now then, there was snow piled on the windowsill, and the window frame was of ebony, which is a shining black wood, and the queen was stitching and dreaming and smiling. She was going to have a baby soon, and when she happened to prick her finger and a drop of crimson blood fell on the shining snow, she looked at it and made a smiling, dreaming wish:

I wish I could have a baby girl, with crimson lips and skin as white as snow and hair as dark as ebony.

'And not long afterwards, her wish came true. She did have a baby girl, and the baby did have hair as dark as ebony and crimson lips and fair, pale skin, and they named her Snow White.'

'That's a funny name.'

'It wasn't unusual in those days. There were all sorts of names that you don't hear now. Rose Red! Briar Rose! I knew a girl called Beauty!'

'Was she beautiful? Was she the most beautiful?'

'She was lovely. So brave. She was a putter-upper!'

'What's a putter-upper?'

'She put up with hard things. But back to Snow White, or have you had enough?'

'No, no.'

'Well then, Sophie, I'm sorry to tell you that the young queen died while her baby was still very small.'

'Oh no!'

'And the King married again.'

'What, straight away, the same day?' asked Sophie, astonished.

'No, of course not the same day. Two years later. He married a very, very beautiful witch.'

'You said this story was true,' said Sophie accusingly.

'So it is.'

'There aren't any witches.'

'There were in those days.'

'And witches wouldn't be beautiful.'

'Most witches are (or were) beautiful. That's how they got away with so much. It's quite true, Sophie, that the King, Snow White's father, married a most beautiful witch.'

'Did he do it on purpose? Did he know that she was?'

'I'm sure he didn't, Sophie. Or else why would he have left his little daughter to be brought up by the new queen when he went away?'

'He went away?'

'Yes, on a long journey to a far country, and he never came back.'

'He died too?' asked Sophie.

'Yes. So Snow White was left to grow up with no one but the Witch Queen and the servants in the palace.'

'Were the servants kind to Snow White?' asked Sophie, thinking of the friendly maids and the cheerful footmen at her parents' palace.

'They didn't dare be kind because they were afraid of the Witch Queen. They were very frightened of her, and they knew she hated Snow White. So Snow White grew up very lonely.'

'Was she pretty?' asked Sophie. 'Like her mother wanted?'

'All little girls are pretty,' said her grandmother. 'I've never seen one that wasn't. Yes, Snow White was pretty, but it didn't help her. It made things worse, because the Witch Queen wanted to be the most beautiful one.'

'The most beautiful one in the palace?'

'The most beautiful one in the land.'

'What did the Witch Queen look like?'

'She was tall and very graceful. You know the way a cat moves, all smooth and balanced? She moved like that. And she had dark-gold shining hair, just like honey, and smoke-blue eyes. Her clothes were lovely too, bright jewel colours, jade and amethyst and ruby red. In wintertime she had thick, soft furs. Sleek, dark otter furs and soft silver-fox furs and dappled snow leopard.'

Sophie shuddered. Furs. The dead skins of animals. But perhaps in those far-off days, a queen had no choice. Perhaps the Witch Queen had to wear furs, just as her own mother had to wear a crown.

'No,' said her grandmother firmly, when she suggested this. 'The Witch Queen *liked* to wear furs. She had huntsmen bring them to her.'

'Oh,' sighed Sophie, turning the crystal in her hand.

'But we were talking about her beauty. She was the most beautiful in the land, and she knew this for certain because she had a wonderful mirror. It had been made hundreds of years before, in the days of deep enchantments. This mirror was her most precious thing, and it was still magic, although it was beginning to grow a little dim.'

'What was its magic?' asked Sophie.

'It always told the truth.'

'That's not magic! So do all mirrors!' objected Sophie.

'Do they? Anyway, this one had a voice. When the Witch Queen looked into it and asked:

Mirror, mirror on the wall
Who is the fairest of them all?

'The mirror would reply:

Queen, you are the fairest of them all.'

◇

Then there was a very long silence between Sophie and her grandmother. It was caused by Sophie wondering: *Did I say words like that? I did. Did she hear me? Where did the words come from?*

She glanced up, and found that her grandmother was looking at her.

'Well,' said Sophie's grandmother, 'that's enough stories for now! Let's try a game.' She jumped up, moved a little table over to Sophie's bed, and opened the box of spillikins. They were thin sticks of sweet-smelling cedar wood, as long as a pencils, but much thinner, carved with patterns of leaves and twirls of stars. Two long silver hooks came with them. The game was to take turns lifting the cedar sticks one by one, without moving the rest of the pile. Playing made Sophie feel much better. She won two games, and her grandmother won one, and then her grandmother exclaimed, 'My goodness! The cherry cake!' and ran down to the kitchen. She made very good cherry cake, with almonds in it, and Sophie was glad when she came back saying, 'Just in time!'

'By tomorrow you will feel like eating it!' she promised Sophie. 'Meanwhile I brought raspberry tarts and tea. It's all nonsense, saying young children shouldn't drink tea! I started drinking it at a very young age, and I enjoyed it very much!'

'How young?' asked Sophie.

'Seven. I had it with sugar lumps in it. Would you like sugar lumps in yours?'

The sugar lumps came in a little silver bowl. Sophie had two lumps, and felt very much revived.

'You do have pretty things,' she said to her grandmother, looking at the bowl, and the spillikins box, which was carved like the sticks with patterns of leaves and stars.

'I do,' agreed her grandmother. 'I like pretty things!' And before Sophie's eyes, she folded a sheet of paper into a snow-white swan. 'There's another!' she said, and put it in Sophie's hands.

'Was the Witch Queen's mirror pretty?' asked Sophie, stroking the swan.

'I don't know,' said her grandmother.

'You must! You're telling the story!'

'I'm telling it,' said her grandmother. 'Not making it up. Everything I tell you is true. I never saw the mirror, so I don't know what it looked like. Nobody ever looked into it except the Witch Queen herself. The magic was fading, you see. Even magic doesn't last forever. So she kept it for herself, and she didn't use it often.'

'Only when she wanted a treat?'

'I suppose so.'

'Oh, what a wonderful mirror,' sighed Sophie, chickenpox-speckled, fuzzy-haired, in a crumpled nightdress with raspberry-tart crumbs and a largish splash of tea down the front. 'Don't you wish you could look into it just once?'

'Certainly not!'

'It might say you were the prettiest grandmother!'

'What if it did? Would that make me any better at making paper swans?'

'Wouldn't it make you happy?'

'I already am happy! It wouldn't make me happier. Isn't it good that I remembered the cherry cake in time?'

'You're not being sensible,' said Sophie crossly.

'If the mirror said I was the prettiest grandmother, would it make you love me more?'

'No of course not!' said Sophie.

'Well then, who cares?' said her grandmother. 'Now, watch!' She unfolded the swan and showed Sophie how to fold it again, following the creases. The first time, Sophie needed help; the second time, only the head and neck were difficult; the third time, she managed completely by herself.

'I did it!' she exclaimed, delighted.

'Good girl!'

'Did your grandmother teach you to make things?' asked Sophie.

'I never knew any of my grandparents.'

'Poor you,' said Sophie, patting her hand.

'Thank you. What shall we call the swan?'

'Snow White,' said Sophie. 'What happened to Snow White?'

'Yes, let's get on with the story,' agreed her grandmother. 'An awful bit is coming and I should like to get past it. Snow White! Every year that she lived at the palace, the Witch Queen detested her more. And when the Witch Queen noticed her looking particularly pretty, she would go to her magic mirror. Those were anxious times in the palace! I should have mentioned, Sophie, that the mirror didn't always reply straight away. Often the Witch Queen would stand for a long while in front of it, waiting and listening, and sometimes the reply was very faint, I think because the mirror was so old.

'Well, there came a day, when Snow White was seven years old, when the Witch Queen asked, and the mirror did not reply. Not for hours and hours, while her maids hovered and whispered, and the whole palace felt heavy and waiting. Like the feeling in the air before a thunderstorm breaks.

'At last the mirror spoke, so loud the servants in the next room could hear it:

My Queen, you are still fair, 'tis true
But Snow White is fairer far than you!

'Then the Witch Queen, trembling, shaking, boiling with rage, went looking for Snow White.'

'Is this the awful bit?' asked Sophie, nervously.

'Yes.'

'And is it all still true?'

'Every word. If you are frightened, we can stop.'

'No, no, no!' cried Sophie. 'What did the Witch Queen do? Did she . . . did she . . . kill Snow White?'

'Queens don't kill people,' said Sophie's grandmother. 'They make other people do it for them. The Witch Queen called for her chief huntsman . . .'

'Oh *no!*' groaned Sophie.

'. . . and she said to him, "Take Snow White deep into the forest and kill her. And bring me back her heart afterwards, as proof that you have truly done it." And so the huntsman went and found Snow White.'

'Did Snow White know what was going to happen?' asked Sophie.

'Yes, I'm afraid she did. She had never felt safe in her whole life, and she knew about the furs and the animals, and besides, she saw his knife.'

Sophie shivered.

'The huntsman rode away from the palace with Snow White bundled up in front of him on his horse. Now, the huntsman was not all bad. Although he was quite used to killing animals, he had never dreamed of killing a little girl. He didn't want to either. So when Snow

White begged him to spare her life, and promised she would never try to find the palace again, he let her go, although he was terrified of what would happen if the Witch Queen found out. Remember she had told him to bring back Snow White's heart!'

Sophie's own heart was beating quite hard.

'Well,' continued her grandmother, 'just at the minute when he released Snow White, a young deer came running towards him. And I wish he hadn't, but he killed it and cut out its heart, and that's what he took back to the palace. Snow White saw it all, and then she turned and ran and ran, and when she couldn't run any further, she staggered and stumbled, desperate to get as far away from the palace as she could.

'And at last, not far ahead, she saw evening sunshine slanting down, and then the trees opened out and she found herself in a garden! A garden in the middle of the forest, with sweet peas and onion beds and beans and currant bushes. There were small stone paths, and there were beehives and a hen house and two white goats, and a well and a strawberry bed. And in the middle of the garden there was a little low house, with a roof so close to the ground that the hollyhocks looked down on it. The house had small windows and a chimney in the middle, like this . . .'

With a pencil from her bag, and a piece of white paper, Sophie's grandmother sketched the house in the

forest so quickly and neatly that in less than a minute Sophie saw that the door was arched and set deep in the wall, and the windows were diamond-paned, and the roof had round tiles with moss growing over them. She also saw the spiral of smoke climbing from the chimney, and the grey cat asleep on the doorstep.

'. . . and Snow White found that the door was unlocked,' continued Sophie's grandmother, 'and there was no one inside.'

'Should Snow White have opened the door?' asked Sophie.

'That's a very good question, and I don't know the answer,' said her grandmother. 'All I know is that she did, and she found herself in a small white room, with a stone-flagged floor and a table in the middle. There were seven places set for supper at that table, with seven loaves on seven plates, seven pears, seven slices of yellow cheese, seven pats of butter, and seven glasses of pale gold wine.

'Snow White had had no food that day. So she took a little cheese from each place, and a little butter, and cut a little piece of bread from each loaf.'

'What about the pears?' asked Sophie.

'Snow White didn't touch the pears because she didn't want to cut them and leave them to go brown. Well, after her bread and cheese, she began to look around, and she saw that at the back of the room were seven beds in a row. Small wooden beds with snow-white pillows and snow-white covers, and this is probably something else she shouldn't have done, Sophie, but she did. She climbed into one of them and went to sleep.'

'In somebody else's bed?' asked Sophie.

'Yes.'

'Dressed?'

'Yes.'

'With her shoes on?'

'No, she took her shoes off.'

'Who did the house belong to?' asked Sophie.

'It belonged to seven dwarves, who worked all day in the silver mines deep in the mountains. When Snow White woke up, quite late in the night, there they were, standing in circle looking at her.'

'Were they cross?'

'They were the kindest people Snow White had ever met.'

'What did they look like?'

'Like this . . .' said Sophie's grandmother, her pencil flickering over the paper again, and she drew seven little men all standing in a ring, just as Snow White might have seen them.

'The tallest was smaller than Snow White herself,' she continued. 'And they wore forest colours, brown and green, and they had large clever brown hands, and deep brown eyes. And they all had thick cream-coloured woollen socks, which they had knitted themselves. When they saw Snow White's eyes open they all spoke in turn:

'"Hush, hush!"

'"There, there!"

'"You're quite safe!"

'"It's only us!"

'"Poor little girl."

'"Don't be frightened."

'"Tell us where your home is and we will take you safely back as soon as it is morning."

'"Oh no!" cried Snow White, trembling. "Oh no! Oh please no! Let me stay! I'll do anything if you let me stay! Sweep the floors and make the beds and c-c-cook the supper for when you come home!"

'That made the seven dwarves smile, but when she told them about the Witch Queen and the huntsman and the poor deer with its heart cut out, they shook their heads at such wickedness. "What can we do to help her?" they asked each other, with worried faces. But to Snow White they said, "Go to sleep again now. It's late. Try not to worry. Things always seem better in the morning."

'So Snow White lay down again, and she was soon asleep once more, but all through her dreams she heard the murmuring of the seven dwarves, who had never met a little girl before, never mind had one arrive in their house and offer to cook their suppers.

'However, by morning the dwarves had made up their minds. "Certainly you can stay with us, until we find something better," they said. "But you will often be alone, because for six days of the week we work in the silver mines, away in the mountains. What will you do all day?"

'"Oh," said Snow White eagerly, "lots of things! I can work hard, I promise I can. And I won't be alone because of the cat!"

'The seven dwarves looked at each other and nodded, and they told Snow White that she could sweep and make the beds as much as she liked, and that the cat was called Smoke and would be glad of the company. But, they added, she must stay inside. The garden and all the outdoor things would have to wait until they came home and could be sure she was safe.

'That was how Snow White's life with the dwarves began, and never did they let her know that they could sweep the floor themselves, with much less bumping, and make the beds as smooth as swan feathers, with much less huffing and puffing. And when she learned to cook, they never mentioned blackness or lumps or forgotten salt or sugar, and they tried not to leave her alone. In the first months, a dwarf often stayed home with her, while the others did his work at the silver mine, and on the seventh day they were all home.

'Snow White had never been so happy. The dwarves were great teachers, and as time went on she learned many things: how to bake and plant seeds and the names of the birds and how to knit socks and carve wood and weave rushes into green mats. The dwarves were silversmiths as well as miners, and they taught Snow White a little of their craft, and she learned to use their hammers and polishing gear.

'Years passed by—'

'But but but,' interrupted Sophie, 'you haven't said what happened at the palace after the huntsman took Snow White! Didn't anybody notice?'

'Oh yes. They did. There were many whispers. Snow White was gone, and no one knew where. The

Witch Queen was almost frightened of the way that the servants looked at her. She buried the deer heart in the garden, and not long afterwards the huntsman disappeared. When he was gone the Witch Queen said, "I wonder if he was the reason we lost our dear Snow White."

'The servants had heard rumours of poison and a new grave at the edge of the forest. They looked at her sideways and did not reply.

'It was many months before the Witch Queen uncovered her enchanted mirror and asked the old question. Then for a long time she waited, but the mirror did not reply. The Witch Queen thought its magic had faded at last.

'Years passed at the palace too . . .

'And then the Witch Queen tried one last time:

> *Mirror, mirror on the wall*
> *Who is the fairest of them all?*

'And straight away came an answer, the worst answer of all:

> *My Lady Queen, you are fair, 'tis true*
> *But Snow White is fairer far than you.*
> *Snow White, who lives with the seven little men,*
> *Is as fair as you, and as fair again.*

'Then the Witch Queen knew that the huntsman had deceived her, and that Snow White was still alive, and she could not bear it.'

◇

'*That's* what was happening back at the palace, Sophie,' said her grandmother.

'It was a good thing,' said Sophie thoughtfully, 'that Snow White didn't know.'

'Perhaps.'

'I wonder what will happen next.'

'Next,' said her grandmother, 'you will have a bath with camomile flowers in it to help stop the itching, and then a walk round the garden. You can pick a bunch of lavender and help me feed the chickens, and those things will help you sleep much better tonight.'

◇

All that day Sophie had not had one chance to look at her piece of crystal, but she hadn't forgotten it. As soon as she was tucked up for the night, she got it out again. It lay in her hand, cold and cloudy as a piece of flint, and just as silent too. Sophie found herself apologizing to it, whispering, 'I didn't have any time. I'm sorry it's too dark now. Don't be angry! I thought you were on my side!'

'*You!*' hissed the vicious voice of the neglected fragment of glass, just as she was falling asleep, and all through the night it whispered, '*You you you!*'

It was the first thing she thought of in the morning.

'Oh!' she cried, after the first, horrified stare. 'Oh no! Oh no!'

The glimpses of her face that she saw in the crystal that morning were absolutely hideous. Never ever had she dreamed she looked so bad. When her grandmother came in to see how she was feeling, she pulled the sheet over her head and wouldn't come out.

'I look awful!' Sophie sobbed. 'Why didn't you tell me?'

'Because you don't look awful,' said her grandmother calmly. 'You look exactly how a person with chickenpox is supposed to look!'

'Have you ever seen anyone with chickenpox before?' asked Sophie.

'Of course I have! When your mother was a little girl she had it, and so did both her sisters and all three of the boys and half the maids at the palace. They all had it together, and their friends came to visit, and they had it too.'

'What happened to them?'

'They got completely better.'

'I hate looking like a monster!'

'You don't look like a monster. You look like a talking sheet. In a very few days you will look like your own cheerful self again. Come and have breakfast in the garden.'

'I'll never have a chance to be the prettiest now,' said Sophie miserably.

'Why would you, why would *anyone*, want to be prettiest?' asked her grandmother gently.

'Because then people like them.'

'People like you, Sophie, very much indeed. And love you too. And they would do just as much if you stayed covered in chickenpox forever. Think about the Witch Queen. She was so beautiful.'

Sad sniffs came from under the sheet.

'Did people love the Witch Queen?' asked Sophie's grandmother.

Sophie did not reply.

'There's not much you can do under a sheet,' said her grandmother, after waiting for a long while, 'but at least you can listen to stories. Do you remember where we were up to? The Witch Queen had heard from the mirror that Snow White was still alive. And so she set out to find her. With magic and with evil spells she transformed herself into the form of an old pedlar women with a basket of trinkets to sell. Then she tracked down the house of the seven dwarves deep in the forest and she hid all through a night, watching and planning. The next morning she counted the dwarves out of the house as they set off to work.

'One, two, three, four, five, six, seven! The dwarves came out of the little arched door, waving goodbye to

Snow White and calling, "Now keep the house locked until we come back!"

"'I will, I will!" replied Snow White, and so she did, even when the old pedlar woman came knocking at the window.

"'Will you buy from my basket?" asked the old pedlar woman. "Ribbons and laces! Brooches and bangles! Stockings and scarves of the finest silk!"

"'I mustn't open the door," said Snow White.

"'But surely you can look through the window," said the old woman. "See, I have strings of beads, as blue as forget-me-nots!"

"'Oh!" exclaimed Snow White, peeping out of the window, and quick as a flash the pedlar woman looped the blue bead necklace over her head.

"'Tighten!" she cried.

'Then the necklace tightened and tightened around Snow White's neck, until she crumpled to the ground and was still.

'The pedlar woman laughed when she saw her lying there, and hurried back to the palace before the dwarves got home.

'They arrived in the evening as usual, weary from their long day, carrying their picks and spades.

"'No smoke from the chimney!" said one, when the little house came in sight, and then they were suddenly alarmed and they dropped their tools and ran.

'And there was Snow White, motionless on the floor, with her eyes wide open and her hands to her throat and not a breath moving her body, and the dwarves saw the beads.

'"Quick!" they cried, and cut the necklace and carried Snow White into the cool garden air.

'"Snow White! Snow White!" they called to her, and at last she blinked, gave a great breath and was alive, and the first thing she said was, "Oh, tell me what happened!"

'But the dwarves could not tell her, and Snow White herself could not remember one thing that had happened after waving them goodbye that morning. She had no memory of the old pedlar woman, and she did not recognize the blue beads when the dwarves showed her them.

'"They are evil things," said the dwarves. "There are dark spells on them." And they took them away to make them safe in the mines in the mountains. "No magic is stronger than mountain magic," they told Snow White.

'For a long time after this, there was an ugly black line on Snow White's throat where the beads had pressed. Perhaps that was why it was so long before the Witch Queen found out that she was still alive.

'But find out she did.

'And she made her plans.

'One snowy winter's day a bright-eyed gypsy came

stepping along the dwarves' little path. She carried clothes pegs and charms and bunches of herbs, such as gypsies used to sell in the olden days. When she came to the window beside the door, she knocked and called, "Missy!"

"'I mustn't open the door," said Snow White, looking from the window. "And I have no money for clothes pegs and herbs."

"'No comb for your hair either, I see!" said the gypsy with a laugh. "Look at it hanging, all tangles and tassels! Is that how you live out here in the woods?"

"'Oh!" said Snow White. "But I brushed it this morning!"

"'Brushes are for floors!" said the gypsy. "You should comb your hair! Lean your head from the window and I'll show you."

'So Snow White leaned her head from the window, and the gypsy took a silver comb from amongst her clothes pegs and she ran it deep into Snow White's hair, and Snow White swayed and clutched the windowsill and was sick and faint. No wonder! Each tooth of the comb was laden with venom like the fang of a snake, and the gypsy pressed deeper and deeper.

'And deeper and deeper.

'Until Snow White fell in a heap on the floor.

'There she lay, all the long day, while the freezing air poured in through the window, and the comb stabbed its poison into her head. No wonder the dwarves saw no smoke from the chimney when they came back at the end of the day.

'That time they thought she was dead. Even when the comb was taken away, she lay limp and grey. Far into the night the dwarves worked to save her, with warm blankets and warm drinks and warm spells of their own. They parted her hair and bathed the place where the comb had been, and they rubbed her hands and heated stones for hot-water bottles and at last she opened her eyes and smiled at them. But she couldn't tell them what had happened. Not a trace of memory remained. The dwarves took the comb and destroyed it, but they could not make Snow White well. She was sick and weak all winter, and the dwarves took turns to stay with her. But with the spring came happier times. The summer birds came back to the forest, the bees woke up in their hives, and Snow White was better again.

'"You have been ten years with us," the dwarves told her one summer's day.

'"The ten best years ever," said Snow White, and she looked at them with love.

'Now, dwarf lives and human lives are not the same. Dwarves live like trees, for hundreds of years. In the ten years that Snow White had spent with them, they hadn't changed a bit. But Snow White had changed. She had grown up. If she wasn't careful, she banged her head on the ceiling of the dwarves' little house, and she had to stoop to look out of the windows.

'She was looking out of the window the day the apple woman came.

'"Fine day," said the apple woman, apple sweet with her apple-round cheeks, nodding and smiling through the window.

'"Beautiful," agreed Snow White. "Are you selling apples?"

'"I am, but I see you have apple trees," said the apple woman, looking at the garden. "So I won't try and sell to you. What do you grow?"

'"The two trees by the beehives are Beauty of the Valley," said Snow White, "and the one by the chickens has big green cooking apples." And then, to be friendly, and because it was nice to talk about apples on a summer morning, she asked, "What apples do you sell?"

'"Nothing but Rosabelles," said the apple woman, lifting her basket so that Snow White could see. "Red as roses! There's no apple like them, for beauty or fragrance, and sweet right through to the heart. Taste!" And she cut an apple from her basket in two, and offered one half to Snow White while she bit into the other half herself.

'"Thank you, how lovely," said Snow White, and she bit into her apple without a single thought of trouble.'

◇

'Oh no, oh no, oh no!' exclaimed Sophie, suddenly out from under her sheet, clutching her knees and gazing at her grandmother. 'Oh no! Why didn't Snow White guess? I guessed as soon as the Witch Queen came to the window!'

'But she looked like a pretty, rosy old apple woman,' said Sophie's grandmother.

'It's not what people look like!' said Sophie. 'It's what they *are!*'

'You are absolutely right, Sophie,' said her grandmother. 'I couldn't agree with you more! Now then, what about breakfast?'

'Breakfast? Breakfast!' shouted Sophie. 'What about Snow White?'

'Snow White bit into the apple and sank into darkness,' said her grandmother.

'Until the dwarves came home?'

'This time the dwarves couldn't help her, Sophie. Snow White was quite still when they found her, but there was no bead necklace to cut away, nor comb to take from her hair. They could find nothing wrong at all. Yet heat couldn't warm her, nor air revive her. All their love and tears could not stir her. And so the world became dark for the dwarves as well. For days they could not believe they had lost her. They had loved her for so long, ever since she was seven years old and had arrived at their home so frightened and alone and offered to cook their suppers.'

'This is too sad,' said Sophie.

'It is too sad,' said her grandmother. 'We will hurry to the end of the story. The dwarves couldn't bear to bury Snow White, so they made her a coffin of crystal and silver and they carried it into the forest . . .'

'WHY?' demanded Sophie.

'Where else could they have put it?' asked her grandmother, surprised.

'In the garden,' said Sophie.

'It would have upset Smoke,' said her grandmother. 'And the bees and the chickens and the goats. The forest was best, and they used to go and visit her there and she never changed; she just lay as if she was sleeping.'

'Perhaps she was.'

'No she wasn't. Remember the apple! Well, one day a handsome prince came riding by (don't groan, Sophie!) and saw her, and he fell in love with her there and then.'

'Is this story still true?' asked Sophie, looking very doubtfully at her grandmother.

'Every word, I promise.'

'Go on then!'

'So the next time the dwarves visited Snow White, there was the Prince. And when very special people meet each other, Sophie, they often make friends at once. So it was with the dwarves and the Prince. And the Prince told the dwarves how he loved Snow White, and how he couldn't bear to go away and never see her again. He begged them to let him take her back to his castle on the hilltop, and in the end the dwarves said he could.'

'And Sophie, I can see that you are bursting with remarks, but be patient one minute longer! The dwarves said they would carry Snow White to the castle themselves, and they lifted the coffin, and it joggled and . . . Snow White coughed! She coughed up the piece of poisoned apple that was stuck in her throat, and there she was, alive again!'

'Good GRACIOUS!' said Sophie.

'And she married the Prince and lived happily ever after! Breakfast time at last!'

'What, she didn't go back and live with the dwarves?' asked Sophie, astonished.

'No, but she visited them every year, and they stayed friends forever.'

'And what happened to the Witch Queen?'

'When the mirror told her that Snow White was alive after all her magic, she flew into a terrible rage and picked it up and hurled it across the room. It exploded into a thousand pieces and the largest piece pierced her heart and she died.'

'All because she wanted to be the most beautiful,' said Sophie, sorrowfully. 'That wicked mirror! It killed her in the end. Poor Queen! Poor Witch Queen!'

'What a strange thing to say, Sophie!'

'I used to want to be the prettiest,' said Sophie. 'A long time ago. So I remember how it feels.'

Then she was silent, thinking.

'What happened to the other pieces of mirror?' she asked at last.

'I don't know . . . *Sophie!*'

How had the crystal got into her hand? Sophie didn't

know. But somehow it had, and there was no hiding it from her grandmother this time; there was much too much blood for that.

'*Your hand!*' exclaimed her grandmother, horrified, and rushed her to the bathroom, where she bathed and bound and bandaged and tutted like a chicken.

'It's a horrible bit of glass I found,' said Sophie furiously. 'I thought it was on my side, but it isn't a bit! I'm never going to listen to it again.'

'Listen to it, Sophie? What does it say?'

'It says *You!*' said Sophie. 'It says "*You! You! You!*"'

'I knew you had a secret!' her grandmother said. 'That's what it was!'

'Yes,' said Sophie, and then she and her grandmother both spoke together.

'*It's a piece of the Witch Queen's mirror!*'

◇

'What shall we do with it?' asked Sophie, much later, after breakfast in the garden by the apple trees.

'Get rid of it,' said her grandmother.

'How?'

'I think,' said her grandmother, 'the dwarves would know how to make it safe. Like they did with the beads and the comb.'

'But the dwarves were in the story!' protested Sophie.

'It was a true story,' her grandmother reminded her.

'But you said it was long, long ago.'

'Long, long ago to us, but not them. The dwarves are still there in the forest, Sophie. Wouldn't you like to meet them?'

'Me?' said Sophie, round-eyed and breathless. 'Me?'

'As soon as you are better we will go and ask their help!' said her grandmother. 'That's the thing to do!'

'But how could we ever find them? Even if they are true!'

'Of course they are true,' said her grandmother. 'I've known them since I was seven years old! And as for how to find them, why, I visit every year!'

Sophie gazed at her grandmother. Gazed and gazed and wondered.

'When you were a little girl . . .' she asked huskily, at last. 'When you were a little girl, long, long ago, what did they call you?'

'Long, long ago, when I was a little girl,' said her grandmother, 'they called me Snow White.'

6

The Prince and the Problem
or
The Princess and the Pea

Once there was a prince, and he lived in a stable . . . but before that, there was a prince who lived in a palace.

The palace was in the middle of a forest. It was not a very big palace, but it had a front door and a back door and turrets and a terrace with a peacock who stalked up and down. So it was a proper palace. Perhaps it only seemed small because the forest was so large. It was a forest of oak trees and beech trees and pines and birches and blackberries and foxgloves and bluebells and thin forest grasses that turned golden in autumn.

In the forest lived squirrels and songbirds and beetles and butterflies and great owls and hawks and foxes and wolves. The weather was very snowy in winter and very damp in spring, wonderful in summer, and wild in autumn. Then the wolf packs gathered for their winter hunting, and darkness came early, and the forest paths were hidden under drifts of fallen leaves. It was easy to get lost in the forest at that time of year.

◇

The Prince in the palace had a Problem. He had had it for years, and at first it had not distressed him at all. However, it had grown, as such things often do.

First a little, then a lot, and then quite suddenly it had become so large it shadowed his days and stalked his nights. Also it made him so sulky and rude and bad-tempered that people who met him said, 'That young man certainly has a problem!'

The Prince had been given his Problem on the day of his christening, when he was six months old. It had been an ordinary royal christening, with fireworks and trumpet fanfares and a large white cake with a blue cradle on the top made of sugar icing. They had named him Charming; a traditional name for a prince.

Fairy godmothers had arrived with gifts: the Crimson Fairy had put a bright red teddy bear and a large ruby-handled sword into the Prince's fat pink hands. The Snow White Fairy gave him silver-bladed ice-skates, and the promise of always snow at Christmas. The Queen had thanked them both, removed the sword and the

skates to keep safe for later (no royal blood was shed: she got there in time), admired the teddy bear (it had real ruby teeth) and said how much they would all enjoy the snow. The Prince had behaved perfectly; everyone said so.

Then the third fairy godmother had appeared. She was the Dust Grey Fairy, and she arrived in a cloud of dust with her grey wolves yammering around her.

The Crimson Fairy and the Snow White Fairy rushed to meet her, scattering a snowstorm of rubies and frost. The trumpets blared a fanfare of welcome. The crowd dipped and swayed into bows and curtsies, the Queen curtsying with the rest. But when the six-month-old Prince was carried across to meet the new arrival, he had stared, and then he had reached out his hand and grabbed . . .

'OW!' shrieked the Dust Grey Fairy. 'LET GO!'

'My dear!' exclaimed the Queen, hurriedly handing the Prince to his nurse. 'Are you very hurt? Let me order you some ice!'

'Ice makes me sneeze!' snapped the Dust Grey Fairy. 'Ouch! Ouch! Ouch! What a dreadful child!'

'I'm sure he didn't mean to hurt you! He doesn't understand how to behave!'

'He understands exactly!' said the Dust Grey Fairy angrily. 'He smiled and waved at the Crimson Fairy only a moment ago! He fluttered his eyelashes at the Snow White Fairy and kissed her hand! She told me herself!'

'It is their glittering and glimmering that attracts him,' said the Queen soothingly. 'Remember he is still very young.'

'Not too young to PULL MY NOSE!' said the Dust Grey Fairy, and she closed one eye and squinted down her nose, to see if it was bent.

It was bent.

'NO PRESENT FOR HIM!' said the Dust Grey Fairy. 'I brought one, in a basket, but he doesn't deserve it now! I shall give him a Problem instead!'

'Pray, don't trouble yourself!' begged the Queen, very alarmed.

'I WILL trouble myself!' said the Dust Grey Fairy. 'I shall give him a Problem that will grow and grow until he learns Who's Who and What's What! That's what he needs!'

'I will make sure he understands those things,' said the Queen faintly. 'When he is older.'

'*I* will make sure he understands all those things when he is older!' replied the Dust Grey Fairy, and she glared at the young Prince so ferociously that the Queen was truly shaken.

'You surely won't turn him into a frog?' asked the Queen. (For this had been known to happen in royal families before.)

'Certainly not!' said the Dust Grey Fairy. 'I'm sure he would enjoy it, lurking around the lily leaves waiting to be kissed, but he would learn no manners at all!'

'Nor send him to sleep for a hundred years?'

'That's for girls only,' said the Dust Grey Fairy. 'Boys are lazy enough as it is.'

'True, true,' admitted the Queen.

'So, quite the opposite. I shall give him a problem that will keep him awake! Now listen, when he marries . . .'

'Marries?' asked the Queen, looking down at the Prince, now back in his cradle and busily gnawing his own left foot.

'MARRIES!' repeated the Dust Grey Fairy. 'Please don't interrupt! He must either marry a true princess—'

'Well, of course he must!' the Queen could not help saying.

'OR . . .' said the Dust Grey Fairy, 'put up with the consequences!'

'Is that all?' asked the Queen, after a quite long pause, for fear of interrupting again. 'That's perfectly reasonable. You are quite right! Naturally, since he is a prince, he must marry a princess. It shouldn't be a problem. There are princesses by the dozen in the castles around here.'

'But are they *true princesses*?' demanded the Dust Grey Fairy.

'Is there a difference?' asked the Queen.

'There are princesses and there are *true princesses*,' said the Dust Grey Fairy. 'I will explain to you how to tell the difference. It is important that you understand, because the consequences of not marrying a true princess will be the fall of this palace!'

'Literally or metaphorically?' asked the Queen shakily.

'Literally!' said the Dust Grey Fairy. 'The walls will tumble and the turrets will topple and the roof will slide to the ground!'

Then the Queen forgot the need to be polite and exclaimed, 'I am sorry about your nose (of course) but that is a Bit Much and I think you are overreacting!'

'Overreacting!' shrieked the Dust Grey Fairy, and at once went off in great huff of grey dust without waiting to tell the Queen how to distinguish a *true princess* from the other sort. However, a week or so later, when she had calmed down a little, she sent the Queen a wolf with a message explaining the secret. She also sent a very small grey bag containing the necessary equipment.

Or part of the necessary equipment.

The other part was too large for the wolf to manage. 'And anyway,' wrote the Dust Fairy, still clearly very annoyed, 'I'm sure you have at the palace ten spare mattresses and ten feather beds! My NOSE,' the letter continued, in grey angry letters, 'is still very much SWOLLEN. Please do not forget my words, and teach that Prince some manners before it is too late!'

Of all the fairies, the Dust Grey Fairy was the most powerful. She reached into every corner and she could not be forgotten. No matter how often the palace was swept and rubbed and polished and scrubbed, her dust came back to remind them of her words.

◇

Meanwhile the Queen grew old and the Prince grew up. Princesses came and went. None of them were true princesses. The Queen was very disappointed. The Prince said he didn't care about any of them, true or otherwise. However, they both agreed that the problem given by the Dust Grey Fairy was very bad luck indeed.

The Prince's manners, if anything, grew worse. He was nearly always grumpy, and the times when he wasn't he stared out of his bedroom window, or ran frantically down the stairs, or wandered distractedly through the forest, calling 'Hey!'

Most of the time, however, he was sulking or arguing or slamming palace doors.

◇

The forest grew wilder. Sometimes, even in the royal bedrooms, they heard wolves howling at night. This did not please the servants, and neither did the dust, nor the grumpiness of Prince Charming. They said he was not charming, not at all. All except one of them, who murmured, very quietly to herself, 'He is, to me.'

◇

But what was the use of that, when the Prince had such a Problem?

◇

Sometimes, when the Queen was feeling particularly old, she wrote messages in the dust to the Dust Grey Fairy, such as 'Help!'

◇

There was a princess in the castle on the other side of the forest. Her name was Hatty and she lived with her grandparents. Since her grandparents were very old, Hatty did all the royal duties by herself. She attended parliament and helped with the laws. She visited banks and helped with the money counting. And she popped into hospitals and helped with the medicines. Also she cut the castle grass and scrubbed the mildew off the castle walls and darned the castle flags and hung them straight on their flagpoles. And every afternoon she put on her silk dress, with the green-and-gold stripes, and her gilt crown with the velvet lining, and went up to sit with her grandparents. She read them the newspapers, and listened to their slow stories of long ago. Her grandparents enjoyed telling the stories more than they did listening to the news because they were so very old.

Everything and everyone in the castle was old, except for Hatty and the kitten.

The kitten had bright blue eyes and bright silver fur. Hatty had discovered it one chilly morning, clinging to a lily pad in the middle of the castle moat. From the moment she fished it out, she was enchanted. She was also twice as busy. The prancing, prowling, purring kitten was a reckless explorer. It needed to be rescued from its explorations almost every day.

After it had been rescued it would curl up tidily and go to sleep, looking very small and perfect. But its tail would twitch, and Hatty would guess that it was planning mischief in its dreams.

The old people at the palace said the kitten was trouble, but Hatty loved it.

◇

As the kitten grew older its adventures became wilder and wilder. One grey and stormy evening the Princess glanced out of her tower-room window just in time to see a streak of silver scamper over the drawbridge, cross the castle gardens, and then disappear, like a blown-out star, into the shadows of the forest.

My goodness! thought Hatty, remembering all the tales she had heard of owls and hawks and foxes and wolves, and she raced out of her room and down the long staircase and across the halls and through the front door and over the drawbridge and into the garden, still wearing the green-and-gold dress and the sparkling gilt crown that she had put on to please her grandparents.

Under the forest trees it was very nearly dark, so it was lucky that the castle kitten was so silvery bright. It glimmered like a firefly in front of the Princess, just bright enough for her to see where it was. It scampered very merrily and quickly, deeper and deeper into the forest . . . and after it, ran Hatty.

'Stop!' she called, but it wouldn't stop. It didn't stop for miles, until finally, in a clearing made by the falling of a huge old oak, Hatty managed to pick it up.

Then at last she could pause to catch her breath and look around.

The wind was rising. Black and silver clouds were being blown across the sky. There was moonlight, and then splatters of rain, and then moonlight again. There were also small green stars.

The stars were low down, amongst the tree trunks.

They were stars that blinked.

They were stars in pairs.

They were golden green.

They came closer.

When the Princess saw them, she clutched the kitten, rolled it in a bundle of gold-and-green skirts, and ran. As she ran, the moon was blotted into darkness and the wind rose to a howl and the splatters of rain became a hard, icy deluge. Although not quite hard and icy enough to scatter the wolves. Each time the lightning flashed, their eyes blinked again, and every time they were a little closer.

'Don't worry!' panted Hatty to the kitten as she ran. 'It's only another adventure!'

The kitten purred. Its silvery whiskers were in perfect order. Its small velvet paws were dry. It was as warm as a bundle of sunshine, wrapped in the gold-and-green silk, and it liked adventures. Already that day it had explored the dizziest part of the castle battlements and the shiveriest corner of the cellars. And when things had become too dizzy or shivery, the Princess had arrived and scooped it to safety, just as she always did.

So the kitten was not worried at all, but the Princess was, quite a lot. When at last she saw a glow ahead, she gasped with relief. And then a flash of lightning outlined the palace, and she ran for the front door, and as she got closer she saw that the glow was the door knocker, made of glimmering golden brass.

'Saved!' she cried triumphantly, and grabbed it and knocked: *Bang! Bang! Bang!*

Bang! Bang! Bang!

All the people in the palace who might ordinarily have opened the door were fast asleep in bed. The maid in the kitchen was too far away to hear. There was only the Prince and the Queen.

The Prince sank deeper into the sofa, crossed his boots on a royal silken cushion, and closed his eyes.

'Darling,' said the Queen, poking him with a silver knitting needle. 'There's someone at the door!'

'Oh, I don't think so,' said the Prince, not opening his eyes.

'Banging very hard!' said the Queen.

'It'll be the wind,' murmured the Prince. 'S'been a horrible day. Horrible weather. Horrible everything.

And now you're imagining noises!'

BANG!

'You must be able to hear that!' said the Queen.

'Mmm?' asked the Prince. 'A slight rustle, perhaps. Ignore, ignore, ignore!'

BANG! BANG!

'Charming!' snapped the Queen. 'I am running out of patience.'

'Poor you,' said Prince Charming. 'I'm not.'

BANG! BANG! BANG!

'Darling Charming,' said the Queen. 'Answer the door or I shall be forced to disinherit you!'

The Prince gave her a quick glance to see if she meant it, saw she did, rolled off the sofa, hitched up his royal trousers, and slammed out of the room.

There was the sound of him stamping across the hall. There was a rattle of latches and a sudden icy-cold draught. There was a breathless voice and the Prince replying and the thump of a door slamming shut, and then, in a very short time, the Prince was back on the sofa again, and his boots were back on the cushion.

'Says she's a princess,' he remarked.

'Says she's a princess!' repeated his astounded mother. 'WHO says she's a princess?'

'Girl at the door,' yawned the Prince. 'Don't they all?'

'There was a girl at the door? What have you done with her?'

'Nothing,' said the Prince.

'You surely didn't leave her standing on the doorstep?'

'Well I wasn't going to bring her in,' said the Prince, sleepily. 'She was dripping!'

'Dripping?'

'Mmm.'

'Dripping *what*?' demanded the Queen. 'Diamonds? Pearls? Blood?'

'Dripping wet,' said the Prince peevishly. 'It's coming down in buckets.' And then he snuggled into the sofa and gave a small but meaningful snore.

'Really!' said the Queen, once more using her silver knitting needles to help the Prince stay awake. 'For all you know you've left a *true princess* drowning on the doorstep!'

'You and your true princesses!' groaned the Prince.

'You've got to marry sometime!'

'Yeah, yeah,' said the Prince.

'Charming, you forget you have a Problem!' said his mother.

'I don't EVER forget I have a Problem!' snapped the

Prince. And with that, he went slamming out of the room.

He exaggerates *everything*! thought the Queen, but just in case, she went and opened the front door and peered out into the storm.

But there was no one there.

◇

When nobody answered her knocking, the Princess did not wait. Nor was she downhearted. She had crossed the wolf-hunted forest. She had survived the storm. She had the silver kitten safe and dry. She was not going to be defeated by a closed front door. Besides, she knew that even the smallest palace has a back door as well as a front. So she set off to find it, staying close to the dark rainy walls, and holding the kitten very tightly. And presently, after several corners and buttresses and leaking gutter pipes, she came to the kitchen. There she saw a dim glow of firelight shining in the window and a slender shadow wavering against a whitewashed wall.

Perhaps because the shadow was so slender and so wavering, perhaps because the fire glow was so dim, this time the Princess did not bang on the door. Instead she put her mouth to the keyhole and called, 'Cooee!'

At once the wavering shadow jumped, a swirl of shadow hair spun, and a voice gasped, 'Oh!'

'It's just me!' called the Princess reassuringly. 'And my kitten!'

But evidently the shadow belonged to a person as brave as the Princess herself, because already the door was open, and there was a girl in a white nightgown saying, 'Please come in.'

◊

So there they were, the Princess laughing and dripping on the doormat, the girl smiling, and rushing for a towel, and the firelight making the puddles glow like pools of copper and bronze and gold.

Then the door was closed and the kitten wriggled free and leaped to the hearthrug, and the Princess's crown was put to drip in the sink and her shoes by the fender, and the Princess herself was wrapped up in a tablecloth.

'Wait!' said the girl. 'I'll lend you my dress!'

In hardly any time after that, the silk gown was

steaming on the clothes horse by the fire and the Princess was sitting on a kitchen stool, dressed in a shabby brown frock.

'Thank you,' she said. 'I'm Hatty.'

'I'm Meg,' said the girl. 'I'm the maid.'

'Were you going to bed?' asked Hatty, looking at Meg's nightgown. But Meg said no, she had crept downstairs to the fire so as to be able to mend her brown dress before morning, and she showed Hatty where she had sewn it, very neatly, and put a pocket over the darn.

'You would hardly know it was torn,' said Hatty admiringly, and then she showed Meg how she had straightened out one of the points on her crown and replaced a lost ruby with a little painted pebble, and Meg said that she could barely tell the difference.

'I didn't know crowns could get worn out,' she said.

'They get bent when they fall off,' Hatty told her. 'They fall off a lot if you don't tie them on with string or something, and of course the jewels get loose with all the bumps. Mine is a very old crown; at least two hundred years. It belonged to seven people before me.'

This explanation made Meg, whose dress was only four years old and had only belonged to one person before her, feel quite well dressed and confident, and she asked, 'Please may I stroke your kitten?'

'Of course. Do you like cats?' asked Hatty.

'I love them,' said Meg. 'There used to be a cat at the

orphanage when I was little. A very old cat . . .' Then she swallowed and blinked back a tear and Hatty lifted the silver kitten and put it on to her lap and after that they were friends forever, best friends.

And so, of course, they began to explain their lives to each other, starting there in the kitchen and working backwards through time, to Hatty's castle, and Meg's orphanage ('I left five years ago next Wednesday,' said Meg) and all the stages in between of dusting and grass-cutting and grandparents and kittens and door knockers and the wolves in the forest and the beetles in the kitchen and the Prince at the front door.

'His name is Charming,' said Meg.

'Prince Charming?'

'Yes. Did you like him?'

'Well,' said Hatty doubtfully, 'I'll tell you what happened. I knocked and knocked and he opened the door at last and I said, "Hello, it's me, Hatty from the castle," and he said, "Who from the what?" and I said, "Princess Hatty from the Old Stone Castle," and he said, "No thank you! Not today!" and shut the door!'

'Oh,' said Meg, and dropped her head to hide a smile in the kitten's fur. 'A lot of princesses come here to the palace,' she continued, after a pause. 'The Queen invites them. There is even a special princesses' bedroom. It has a golden bedroom door, and no one but princesses are ever allowed to go in, not even to make the bed.'

'Who does make the bed, then?' asked Hatty.

'The Queen, I think,' said Meg. 'The Queen is very particular about everything to do with princesses. I don't know what she would say if she knew I had one here in the kitchen!'

'Perhaps I'd better tell her I'm here,' said Hatty, seeing Meg's suddenly worried face. 'What about the kitten? Will she mind the kitten? Does she like cats?'

'She hasn't got cats,' said Meg, thinking aloud. 'She likes diamonds and she has diamonds, and she likes yellow lilies and she has yellow lilies, and she likes green shoes and she has green shoes, but she hasn't any cats so I think perhaps she doesn't like cats, because Queens can have anything they like, can't they?'

Hatty said, yes, probably some of them really could, and since the kitten was asleep she would leave it with Meg, if Meg didn't mind, and Meg said of course not, she loved it. Then they both looked at Hatty's shoes, which had become quite sodden during her journey through the forest, and Meg offered to lend her her boots, but Hatty said, no need, she would explain to the Queen, and bare feet were quite comfortable indoors.

◇

And so the Princess, barefoot and empty-handed, with her hair dangling down her back in damp strings, made her way from the kitchen by long chilly corridors to the royal sitting room at the front of the castle. There she found the Queen putting away her knitting and feeling very old.

'And who are you?' asked the Queen, after Hatty had made a rather shivery curtsy in her cold bare feet.

'I'm Hatty from the castle,' said Hatty. 'I got lost in the forest for hours and hours and at night it grew dark and there were wolves.'

'Well of course it grew dark at night!' said the Queen severely, after looking at Hatty from top to toes. 'And naturally there are wolves! Very careless of the castle, to let their maids go running around the forest willy-nilly! What were they thinking of to allow it?'

Hatty explained about being a princess, not a maid, and therefore allowed to do anything she pleased, and the Queen looked at Meg's old brown dress with the pocket over the darn and sniffed and said, 'I see.'

Dust specks floated in the lamplight.

'Well,' said the Queen, remembering her manners as she watched them, 'there *was* somebody knocking, and my son *did* say something about a princess! I thought he must be mistaken . . .'

Once more she looked doubtfully at Hatty, but then again at the dancing dust.

'. . . but perhaps not,' she continued. 'Anyway, it's very late and I'm sure you must be tired.'

'Very tired,' agreed Hatty.

'Then you must go to bed. We have a spare room that

we keep especially for . . . er . . . princesses. The bed is made, I did it myself, and the room is all aired and dusted.'

Hatty, very much cheered at the thought of any bed at all, replied that she did not mind dust in the least, and that parts of the castle where she lived were very dusty indeed.

'I'm sure they are,' said the Queen, and despite her good intentions she glanced down at Hatty's feet.

'The forest,' said Hatty apologetically, 'was muddy.'

'Ah,' said the Queen. 'Never mind. Here we are!'

All this while, she had been leading Hatty upstairs and along corridors. Now she paused at a golden door, and took a key from the chatelaine she wore at her waist.

'I think you will find everything you need!' she said, as she turned it in the lock. And before Hatty could murmur politely that all she really needed was a bed, she found herself being pushed gently into a shadowy room, lit by a small lamp hanging high amongst the rafters.

'Goodnight!' said the Queen, and then Hatty was alone.

◇

So there was Hatty, in the most surprising room that she had ever seen.

The astonishing thing, and the *only* thing, about the bedroom was the bed. There was absolutely nothing else in the place, not a chair, or a table, or a window seat, or even a mat. Except for the bed and the bare floor, there was no other possible place to sleep.

It was an absolutely staggering bed. It stood all alone in the middle of the room, and Hatty walked around it and around it, staring.

The bed had layer after layer of mattresses, in all different patterns of stripes, and layer after layer of feather quilts, in every colour of the rainbow. Hatty counted them: ten striped mattresses, ten bright feather quilts.

The other thing the bed had was a ladder. That was because the mattresses and quilts made it so high above the floor. Higher than Hatty's head, quite close to the ceiling rafters.

After some time of gazing at this bed, Hatty went to the bedroom door and opened it. Dark corridors stretched in both directions. There was not a sound to be heard.

Hatty looked back at the bed.

After a while, she climbed the ladder.

There were pillows at the top, and a golden coverlet that matched the door. Hatty pulled it over herself, and lay down very carefully.

Then she sat up and looked over the edge.

The floor looked very far away.

◊

This room, thought Hatty, a long time later, is lonelier than the forest.

She had left the door a little bit open. She wondered if she would feel better if it was shut. She climbed down the ladder and closed it, and then, after a few minutes of sitting in bed, looking at it closed, she climbed down once more and opened it again.

Then she went back to bed.

She was sure she could hear something. The tiniest sound in the world, but very nearby. A tiny, very close, scratchy sound.

Sometimes Hatty was sure she could hear it. Sometimes not. And there was something about that small sound, in that empty room, that was very worrying.

Just as Hatty had reached a point when she could not bear it any longer, and could not face the dark corridors either, something absolutely wonderful happened . . .

The kitten arrived. And, even more wonderful, after the kitten came Meg.

'Oh Meg, oh Meg, oh Meg!' cried Hatty, tumbling down the ladder to hug her. 'Oh thank goodness!'

'I had to come!' said Meg. 'The kitten woke up all of a sudden and ran! Fancy it finding you, down all those corridors! WHATEVER . . .' she asked, emerging from the hug to blink and stare, 'kind of a bed is THAT?'

And she burst out laughing, and with Meg's laughter everything became suddenly and brilliantly much better.

'I KNOW!' agreed Hatty. 'LOOK at it! Ten stripy mattresses and THEN ten feather quilts!'

'The kitten likes it,' said Meg. And it was true that the kitten was having a very joyful mountaineering time, exploring the bed. It didn't need a ladder to race up and down the quilts and mattresses. It hung on with its claws and dodged when Hatty tried to pick it up, and then sat at the top, purring and twitching its tail.

'Please can I go up too?' asked Meg.

'Of course you can! I'll come after you. There's plenty of room, but look how far away the floor is! Do you think people ever fall out?'

'They must,' said Meg. 'I would.'

'I will,' said Hatty with conviction. 'I'm sure I will, if I go to sleep. I nearly did before you came. I was lying here listening . . . Meg, there's something making a sound, a tiny sound, like nearly nothing . . . anyway, I was trying to listen and my eyes must have closed just for a moment without me noticing and when I opened them again I was right at the edge of the bed. The trouble is, I'm so tired.'

'Go to sleep,' suggested Meg. 'I'll stay awake and make sure you don't fall out.'

'What about you?'

'Then you can stay awake and make sure that I don't.'

'Promise to wake me up and take turns fairly?'

'Promise,' said Meg. 'And I'll listen for the noise you

heard, now the kitten is quiet.'

The kitten, having prowled round and round, and climbed up and down, and dived into the pillows and scrabbled under the golden coverlet, had settled down at last. It curled between the girls like a small silver cloud, very warm and comforting.

The kitten slept, and so did Hatty, and soon Meg's eyes began to close too.

The tiny sound began again.

A very

small

squeak . . .

'Hatty!' cried Meg, jerking awake, and Hatty jumped in her sleep, rolled over, and grabbed a bedpost just in time to stop herself falling right out of bed.

'I forgot where I was,' she gasped. 'What is it?'

'A mouse!'

'A mouse?'

'I heard a mouse, right here!'

'Right where?'

'Right here in this bed!'

It was strange that although Hatty could manage wolves in the forest and Meg could manage beetles in the kitchen, neither of them could quite bear the thought of a mouse right there in the bed. They each knelt clutching a pillow and gazing at the other, tense with listening, and when the sound came again, quite clearly a squeak, they both toppled backwards at exactly the same moment.

The floor was just as far away and painful as they had expected it to be.

'Oh! Oh! Oh!' gasped Meg.

And Hatty groaned. 'Ouch, ouch, ouch, I am bumped all over!'

They were both banged and bruised, but the kitten, who had jumped down after them, was not hurt at all. The kitten was dancing with excitement.

'It knows there's a mouse,' said Meg.

And Hatty agreed, and she caught the kitten and tied it in a pillowcase before any awfulness could happen. And then she said, 'I'm definitely not going back up that ladder again.'

'Neither am I,' said Meg.

'And why would there be a mouse in the bed anyway?'

'Looking for food,' said Meg. 'That's what mice do. Perhaps the princesses have breakfast in bed and drop crumbs.'

'Oh no!' said Hatty. 'But that can't be true! The Queen makes the bed! She said so! She would sweep out the crumbs in the morning!'

'Queens don't know much about sweeping,' said Meg.

'You don't think she just puts another layer on top?' asked horrified Hatty.

'Perhaps she does, and that's why there are so many.'

'Then all those mattress and quilts are just crumb sandwiches!' said Hatty.

They both gazed at the bed, and it seemed even less inviting than before, and while they were gazing, they heard squeaking again, squeaking and scrabbling, quite definitely.

'It *is* a mouse,' said Hatty. 'It's a mouse in that highly dangerous, mousey, giant crumb-sandwich bed! I won't be able to sleep a single wink until I've taken it all to pieces and shaken all the crumbs out the window!'

'I'll help you,' said Meg.

'We'll have to put it back together again afterwards,' said Hatty.

'Of course,' said Meg.

So then Hatty and Meg set to work.

And it took ages and ages.

Because the feather beds were very puffy.

And the mattresses were very heavy.

And the whole thing was very puzzling to Hatty and Meg, because there were not any crumbs.

Only, towards morning, as they lifted the very last mattress of all, a very big grey mouse darted out and escaped away through the open window.

And under that last mattress Hatty and Meg found three large dried peas, slightly chewed.

◇

When the Queen, tiptoeing along the corridor in the early morning to find out how the Princess had slept through the night, paused outside the golden bedroom door, she was astonished to hear voices.

Girls' voices, two of them.

Very softly, the Queen pushed open the door.

There was the bed, looking just as she had left it, but also, to her great bewilderment, there were two girls, where the night before she had only left one. Two brown-haired girls with their backs to her, examining something in the early-morning light at the window. One wore a shabby brown dress that she recognized from the night before. The other wore a white nightgown, rather too small.

'Peas!' she heard the brown-dressed girl exclaim. 'Dried peas! Now I understand why I hardly slept a wink! How do you suppose they got there?'

'That mouse must have carried them all the way from the kitchen,' said the white-nightgowned girl. 'If it *was* a mouse! It looked so big that perhaps it was even a ra—'

'Don't say it!' begged the brown-dressed girl. 'Oh, what an awful night! I am black and blue with bruises! How could anyone sleep in a bed like that?'

I've found her! thought the Queen with joy. *I've found a True Princess at last! But who is the other girl?*

She would have gone in to ask, if at that moment she had not heard the unmistakable slam of Prince Charming's bedroom door, far along the corridor, followed by the equally unmistakable swish of him sliding down the banister towards the front hall, clearly intent on avoiding breakfast and princesses if he possibly could.

'Charming!' called the Queen, speeding to the top of the stairs.

'Oh, hullo, Ma,' said Prince Charming, his hand already reaching for the doorknob. 'Just popping out!'

'Not when we have a guest for breakfast!' said the Queen, hurrying down to the hall.

'Oh, do we?' said the Prince, unenthusiastically.

'We do!' said the Queen, getting firmly between him and the doorknob. 'And darling Charming, listen! I think your Problem is solved at last!'

The Prince could not have looked less thrilled if he had turned into a frog, and he followed his mother most reluctantly into the dining room, which was in such a state of dustiness that morning that for some time he could do nothing but sneeze.

'Don't!' begged his mother, although sniffing dreadfully herself. 'Look at the state of this room! Where is the maid this morning?! Now, don't just stand there sneezing, Charming! Do something useful! Dust!'

'All right,' said the Prince, with most unusual

helpfulness. 'I'll just dash to the kitchen for a duster!'

'No!' exclaimed his mother. 'Don't go ANYWHERE! Any moment she will be here! Oh!'

It was Hatty, and since the Queen had last seen her, she and Meg had been very busy. Hatty was once more in her silken stripes, now dried and ironed by Meg, her hair was smoothly tucked under her sparkling gilt crown, her bruises were hidden under her green-and-gold sleeves, and she was at her most princessly polite, even when the Prince greeted her by saying, 'Oh. You got in then?'

'Yes,' she agreed, and curtsying beautifully to the Queen, added, 'Thank you so much for having me.'

'A pleasure,' said the Queen, wondering who in the world she was, but helplessly good-mannered in return. 'You met my son last night?'

'On the doorstep,' said Hatty, curtsying again, this time to the Prince.

She was definitely a princess, thought the bewildered Queen, but what kind of a princess? And where had she come from? And most important of all, where was the shabby, brown-dressed, *true princess*, who she herself had shown to bed the night before, and overheard that very morning, saying quite plainly that she was bruised all over and had hardly slept a wink because of the three dried peas!

'You slept well?' asked the Queen, staring in confusion.

'On and off,' said Hatty, rubbing her bumped elbows. She did not mention, as no true princess would, dried peas or mice or rats, but the Queen looked so put out at her reply that Hatty could not help asking, 'Is something wrong?'

'No, no,' said the Queen. 'Well. Yes. And no. It's just that we thought the Prince's Problem was solved at last and now it seems . . . OH, THERE SHE IS!'

With these words the Queen rushed out of the room, leaving Hatty staring in surprise at the Prince. The Prince said nothing, but kicked a table leg so moodily that she asked, 'What *is* the matter?'

'Oh, she was hoping I would marry you, that's all,' said the Prince grumpily.

'NO!' exclaimed Hatty, shocked into impolite honesty. 'What an awful idea!'

'Don't worry, I'm not going to.'

'Neither am I,' said Hatty with feeling.

'She thought you were a true princess, that's why. It's because of my Problem.'

'What is your Problem?'

'I'll tell you if you promise not to marry me,' said the Prince. And Hatty promised most sincerely, straight away, and in return she heard about the christening of the Prince, and the Dust Grey Fairy, and the need for a true princess to teach the Prince who was who, and what was what. She also heard about the peril of the palace tumbling to ruin if the Prince should marry anyone who was not a true princess, and how this terrible Problem had shadowed his life for years and years.

'How many years?' asked Hatty.

'Five next Wednesday,' said the Prince. 'That's how long I've known M—' He stopped abruptly. 'Oh, never mind!'

Hatty looked at him thoughtfully, and instead of demanding, 'Known who?' asked instead, 'And what if the palace did fall down?'

'What?' exclaimed the Prince.

'And what if the palace did fall down?' repeated Hatty.

'Say that again!' said the stupefied Prince.

'What,' said Hatty patiently, 'if you married someone who was not a true princess and the palace did fall down?'

'Then,' said the Prince, after blinking quite a lot, 'I wouldn't have a palace.'

'But,' said Hatty, 'you wouldn't have a Problem.'

Dust shimmered in the sunlight.

The Prince stared at Hatty. He stared at the windows and the ceiling. He strode out of the dining room and across the hall and on to the terrace, where he stood back and held his hands to shade his eyes and stared at the turrets.

'I suppose we could live in the stables,' Hatty heard him murmur. And then he stared some more at the tiles and the walls and the buttresses, and while he was still doing this the Queen came hurrying across the garden with Meg in her old brown dress.

'I've found her! I've found her!' cried the Queen. 'And she is a perfect darling and she didn't sleep a wink and you should see her poor bruises and she still has the peas in her pocket and you absolutely must marry her, Charming! Why are you staring at the roof like that?'

So Prince Charming stopped staring at the roof and he turned round and looked.

'Why, Meg!' he said in a voice that no one except Meg had ever heard before.

◇

That was how the Prince at last learned from a true princess who was who, and what was what. He became very joyful, and so did Meg. And Hatty gave them the silver kitten for a wedding present. What was even better and kinder was that she took the Queen back to her own castle for a very long visit while the Prince and Meg got used to living in the stables. The Queen loved living at Hatty's castle. Everyone there was so old that in no time she found herself feeling very young indeed.

The Prince and Meg found the stables quite comfortable, hardly dusty at all. In time, they grew roses over the ruins of the palace, and whenever the Dust Grey Fairy came to visit they gave her a bunch to take home.

And they all lived happily ever after.

7

Over the Hills and Far Away

or

Red Riding Hood and the Piper's Son

There was a village, with a forest behind it, close behind, like a shadow. The village had an inn, and the inn had a doorway, and the doorway had a doorstep, and one winter's morning there was a parcel on that doorstep.

You can't leave a parcel on a doorstep for long. Not if it's alive. So they took it in, the innkeeper and his wife, and they brushed off the frost and unknotted the string, unfolded the shabby brown blanket, and there was a baby.

'It's not from round here,' said the innkeeper's wife at once.

'Gypsy,' said the innkeeper.

'Gypsies have black eyes.'

'Green-eyed gypsy,' said the innkeeper. 'Boy or girl?'

'Girl,' said his wife, unfolding the blanket further. 'Look! Gold earrings!'

'Never!'

'See for yourself!' his wife replied. So the innkeeper bent and looked, and sure enough, the baby had gold earrings under its wisps of brown hair.

'Someone will be back for it,' said the innkeeper. 'One thing to leave a baby on a doorstep. Another to leave gold earrings.'

'I shall say what I think when they come!' said his wife. 'Leaving it there for anyone to trip over! Half frozen too.'

The baby's wide green eyes looked at her. It didn't cry. They found out later that it hardly ever cried.

They gave it bread and milk, and a warm basket by the stove. No one ever came back for it, and so it stayed, from day to day, and then from week to week, and eventually from year to year. The innkeeper and his wife got paid a little for keeping it instead of sending it away to the orphanage. They called the baby Polly.

'A good plain name,' they said, looking disapprovingly at Polly's ears. Although they had both tried, they could find no way of taking off the earrings without taking off the baby's ears too. So the earrings also stayed. Perhaps if they had come off, they would have liked Polly more than they did; but perhaps not, because Polly was different. She was not like any child that had ever been in the village before, nor any grown up either. For one thing, Polly was not afraid of the forest.

The forest curved around the village like a heavy, green, growing threat. To the villagers it was like living on the borders of a dangerous unknown world. Except for gathering firewood on its borders, they avoided it. Some of the forest dangers were real: falling branches from ancient trees, hidden pits dug in the bad old days for animal traps, the possibility of being lost forever. Some dangers were less certain. The villagers were almost sure there were no bears, but also almost sure there really were wolves. There were probably no witches and certainly no dragons, but there were brambles like tripwires and poisonous mushrooms. The owls were eerie, large bats swept from its borders at night to hunt over the fields, while small, amber-eyed foxes slipped from bone-littered dens and returned with fat chickens clamped in their jaws.

Polly said, 'I like foxes better than chickens.'

The village children who heard this were not shocked, as they would have been if one of them had said it themselves. They did not think of Polly as one of them. Even after living all her life in the village, her newness had not worn off. The innkeeper's wife dressed her exactly like the other village girls, in pale browns, and greys and blues, thick boots for winter, sun hats for summer, but she did not look like the other girls. They were blue-eyed and sunny-haired, with sturdy legs and freckled noses. They played with raggy dolls in homemade dresses, made houses under willow trees, read and re-read their few battered storybooks, gathered flowers in floppy bunches and arranged each other's hair. Polly could not seem to join in with their games. Her straight brown hair was not interesting to comb, and her doll lay in its wooden cradle for months on end without being disturbed.

Until it died, her favourite companion had been the inn's ancient ginger cat. She had been lonely for a while after it was gone, until the innkeeper bought a small black pig for the sty at the end of the garden.

'I could look after it!' Polly offered eagerly.

'I don't think so,' said the innkeeper. 'No. You should help in the kitchen.'

Polly did help in the kitchen, as often as she could, which was not very often because the innkeeper's wife liked things done her own way, by herself. Polly bothered her, with her quickness and her differentness and her golden earrings. Often the innkeeper and his wife thought of the day when they had opened the door and taken the parcel that was Polly inside. They wondered about the orphanage.

'There's nothing to stop us sending her there yet,'

said the innkeeper's wife.

'Nothing at all,' said the innkeeper. 'And you should keep her away from that pig.'

'She slips off,' said his wife.

So at breakfast the next day the innkeeper himself told Polly, 'Now don't go getting fond of that pig!'

'Diamond!' said Polly, between spoons of porridge. 'I call him Diamond! Diamond Pig!'

'Eh?'

'Because he is precious, like a diamond!'

'You leave him be now, Polly. You play with that doll. Pigs don't have names.'

'Why not?'

'Pigs are pigs.'

'Of course they are.'

'It's easier in the end.'

'Easier for what?' asked Polly.

The innkeeper was eating sausages and did not wish to continue the conversation, so he said, 'Finish your porridge now, Poll!'

'I have. Why—'

'And no more talk about that pig.'

'Diamond.'

'Is she like this all day?' the innkeeper asked his wife. 'Bothersome?'

'Oh,' said Polly. 'I didn't know I was bothersome.'

'Well, now you do,' said the innkeeper's wife.

'Bothersome! Now take a broom and off outside to get the inn yard swept!'

Polly the Bothersome swept the yard, tiptoed down the garden path to give a private hug to Diamond, and then wandered on to the village street, where a group of girls were gathered, pulling petals from a daisy.

'Why're you doing that?' she asked.

'Seeing who we'll marry,' they said, friendly enough. 'What've you been doing, Polly?'

'Sweeping,' said Polly.

'There's a smell . . . Sniff your dress, Poll! Sniff your hands!'

Polly sniffed and said, 'Oh! I know! That's Diamond!'

'What's Diamond?'

'The innkeeper's new little pig,' explained Polly. 'I called him Diamond. He's black. He's lovely. He lets me hug him!'

The whole group of girls burst into laughter. 'Hug him!' they exclaimed. 'Hug a pig!'

Polly looked at them. They had fathers and mothers and little brothers and sisters to hug. Dogs and cats and grannies and grandpas. They shouldn't laugh, just because she had only a pig.

However, they did laugh, and so did the boys when the girls told them. The biggest boy, Tom Piper, the only person in the village who might have understood, laughed most of all. Tom was no blue-eyed, round-faced village boy. Tom's parents were dead and he lived with his uncle, a rough tough farmer who made Tom earn his keep. Tom did not have a proper home any more than Polly did. He need not have said, 'And did you kiss the pig too, Polly?'

'No she didn't!' cried several of the girls protectively. 'Shut up, Tom!'

'She did; she's blushing!' said Tom.

'You didn't, did you, Polly?'

'Only between his ears!' said Polly.

'Polly!' exclaimed the girls.

'Polly!' mocked Tom, his teeth showing in a white grin.

'Shut up!' Polly aimed a kick at his shins. 'You're just like the innkeeper! He doesn't want me to like Diamond either.'

'Diamond?' asked Tom, grabbing and holding her at arm's length so she couldn't kick again. 'The innkeeper called his pig Diamond?' he asked, his grin wider than ever.

'*I* called him Diamond!' said Polly. 'The innkeeper said he shouldn't have a name.'

'Why not?'

'Because he doesn't love him.'

'Oh dear. But do you love him, Poll?'

Polly turned her face from his laughter. The girls pulled his arms and said, 'Let her go now, Tom.'

'She'll kick me.'

'She won't, will you, Polly?'

'I might,' said Polly. But when Tom let her go, she didn't. Instead she asked, 'Why shouldn't pigs have names?'

The girls murmured uncomfortably, eyeing Tom, wondering if he would tell.

Tom said, 'Show me this pig!'

'No,' said Polly.

'They bite, you know.'

'He never would,' said Polly scornfully.

'How big is he?' asked one of the girls.

Polly held her hands apart to show that Diamond was about as big as the ginger cat had been.

'Plenty of time then,' said Tom, sauntering away.

'Time for what?'

'Kisses!' called Tom, over his shoulder, and he closed his eyes and made kissing, grunting sounds until all the girls were giggling again.

Polly ran away from them, stumbling in her clumsy boots until she took them off to walk barefoot. At the edge of the forest she pulled them on again. That was not the place for bare feet: not only were there thorns and rough ground, but also the villagers had a habit of dumping their unwanted rubbish at the forest edge. Broken pots, rags, house waste and farm waste, a dead cat now and then.

Polly picked her way through carefully, following the path. She had been that way before once or twice; it led to a sheltered hollow amongst the trees, and then on to an old cottage, hardly more than a mile from the last of the village houses, but still too far for most people. In the past, Polly had never been further than the hollow, but this time she walked on, into the deeper green darkness under the trees.

That was the first time Polly visited the old woman that the village called Granny.

Polly, dressed in faded blue with muddy patches from the pig, did not show up at all amongst the forest shadows. Granny jumped with shock when she suddenly appeared in her open doorway.

'Goodness, child!' she exclaimed. 'Creeping up on me like that!' And she turned quickly to a chest in the corner of the room, but not so quickly that Polly did not see as the lid closed down.

'Oh!' exclaimed Polly.

'Oh, what?' asked Granny crossly, for in the chest were various things that she had acquired throughout her long and exciting life. Surprises from shipwrecks, gifts from grateful smugglers, and a few bright sparkles of pirate treasure, for Granny had once lived by the sea.

Polly did not glance at the brandy flasks or the things that sparkled, but what she *did* notice was a most beautiful glowing redness, and she cried out as the lid went down, 'Oh, please, let me look again!'

'Look at what, my dear?' asked Granny, alarmed.

'The red,' said Polly.

And then Granny laughed and took from the chest a piece of ruby-red, glowing red, gorgeous red, woven cloth. The clearest, brightest, most-singing piece of colour that Polly had ever seen.

'That would just make a nice red riding cloak for you!' said Granny, when Polly had rubbed it, and sniffed it, and laid her cheek on it, and adored it.

'For me?'

'Why not?' Granny draped it round her shoulders and stood her in front of an old, speckled mirror.

'But don't *you* want it?'

'Not as much as you do,' said Granny. And then and there she sat down with scissors and a sewing basket, and before the morning was over, there it was: a glowing red cloak with a wide hood, and a red bow to fasten it, long enough to cover the dull blue dress, right down to Polly's knees.

By the time the cloak was finished, Polly and Granny were friends, and Granny had heard all about Diamond and Tom, while Polly had explored the whole one-roomed house, with its bed in the corner and round table by the fireplace, and the rocking chair and the wooden stool and the window at the back where deer came to be fed.

She had also been useful. While Granny sewed, Polly milked her two white goats, pushed the treasure chest back under the bed, carried in logs for the fire, collected three eggs from the four brown chickens that each had names, and boiled two of them for their tea. Then, wearing her red riding cloak, and very happy, she walked with Granny to the edge of the forest because it was nearly dark and time to go back to the village.

Overhead, the sky was dark purple, and stars were caught in the windblown branches.

'Are there wolves?' Polly asked Granny, as they passed under the spangled trees.

'There are and there aren't,' said Granny.

It was Tom who saw the scarlet cloak first. He bowed low to Polly, sweeping off an imaginary cap. 'Oh, Red Riding Hood!' he exclaimed. 'You look like you are wearing a sunset!'

Polly sparkled with pleasure.

'Where did it come from?'

'Granny in the forest.'

'Is that where you ran off to? Weren't you afraid?'

'No.'

'Not of wolves? Bears? Darkness? The pits under the trees? Not of Granny?'

'No.'

'Gold earrings, red cloak, and nothing frightens you!'

'I didn't say nothing frightened me.'

'Where are you going now, Poll? Back to the inn?'

Polly nodded, her sparkles fading.

'Well, don't go wasting any more kisses on that pig!'

'Shut up, Tom Piper! Stop laughing! Shut up! You spoil everything!'

'Oh Poll, I don't! Poll, I'm not laughing! Oh, Red Riding Hood! I'm just jealous, that's all!'

Tom's name for Polly, *Red Riding Hood*, stuck. The village took it up, half kindly, half as if to say, *You're not one of us.*

Granny's present caused a sensation. The girls gazed and gazed.

'You can put it on if you like,' Polly offered.

And one or two of them did, nervously sliding it round their shoulders, glancing down with their hands to their mouths, shaking it off as fast as they could, saying, 'Oh, it's pretty, but I never could! I never could wear such a colour as that!'

'I should feel such a poppy!' said one.

The fact that it came from Granny in the Forest made them all nervous. Granny visited the village now and then, and although she was old and bent and stiff and wrinkled, there was something about those visits that bothered the villagers.

'I can't abide whispers,' Granny would say, 'and I can't abide fools, and they might as well know it!'

There were a lot of whispers when Granny came into the village, and a lot of people she thought fools, including the innkeeper and his wife. They did not believe in witches, but they did not believe in taking chances either, so when they saw Polly's new cloak they did not say, 'You're not going out dressed like that, Young Lady!'

Although they did say:

'First the earrings, now this!'

and

'You'll scare every horse in the village!'

and

'I suppose it would cut up for dusters.'

and

'Let's hope it fades!'

Polly took no notice of any of these remarks and she wore the cloak every day. It did not fade or scare the horses or get cut up for dusters, and it seemed to make Polly's gold earrings shine even brighter than before. The village got used to it, even the innkeeper and his wife. They also got used to the fact that Polly had a new friend. Very often she set off to visit Granny in the forest, and the innkeeper and his wife (so as not to take chances) now and then sent small presents: a little loaf of bread, a cake or two, some butter or some cheese. In return Granny would send back her own presents: honey, blackberry wine, cold roast pheasant and venison pasties.

So the summer passed. Polly was happy. Diamond grew from a small black piglet to a fat friendly little pig. Polly still hugged him first thing in the morning, and she still kissed him between his ears last thing at night. The village girls still said, 'Polly! You shouldn't!'

'What shouldn't she do?' Tom asked.

'Make such a pet of that pig,' the girls told him.

'He's not just an ordinary pig,' said Polly. 'He's a very clever pig. He knows all sorts of things. If I say, "Speak, Diamond!" he squeaks back at me. And if I say, "Bedtime!" he lies down quiet! And he can dance! He does twirls! I taught him!'

'How big is he now?' asked Tom.

Polly proudly stretched her arms to show how big Diamond had grown.

Tom whistled and said, 'I've got to see this pig!'

'One day,' said Polly.

'One day soon,' said Tom.

'All right,' agreed Polly, pleased at such interest in her beloved Diamond, 'but it will have to be early, early, early in the morning. That's when I teach him things. Before the innkeeper wakes up.'

'Well then,' said Tom, 'that's when I'll be there. Early in the morning tomorrow, so mind you're awake!'

Polly looked at him in surprise. His voice was suddenly cold, not joking any more, and his eyes, looking back at her, were watchful and gleaming. Something was wrong, but what it was Polly could not think, and before she could ask questions, he had turned away.

That night she woke feeling uneasy, without knowing why. She wondered if Tom would be there in the morning.

But Tom did come, and he was his usual self again, calling her Red Riding Hood and grinning as he stalked ahead of her through the long frosty grass. It was a fine morning, the beginning of winter. Polly fed Diamond with apples saved from the orchard, and acorns and beechnuts gathered in the forest, and Tom watched them together, heard Diamond squeak on command

and saw him lie down quiet when Polly said, 'Time for bed!'

'Dance now, Diamond!' whispered Polly.

And Diamond twirled in enchanting, fat black circles.

'Oh you brilliant Diamond!' said Polly, and bent and kissed him between his ears. And when she looked up, Tom was gone.

◇

That was the last time Polly saw Diamond in his sty at the end of the innkeeper's garden, the last time he danced for her in the early morning on his short little sausagey legs. The innkeeper put his pig to bed himself that night, and when Polly ran down the next morning the sty was empty and Diamond was gone.

After one long, horrified stare, Polly turned and ran. Back to the house, up the stairs and then she was hammering on the innkeeper's bedroom door with both fists and shouting, 'Where is he? Where is he? What have you done with Diamond?'

'That girl!' Polly heard the innkeeper's wife exclaim. And then the door was opened and there they both were, as bewildered and angry as Polly herself, especially after they had pulled on boots and coats and gone down the garden to look at the pigsty. They noticed what Polly had not seen: the little gate splintered and wrenched off its hinges, the scattered straw and overturned water trough, and in the mud by the trough

a footprint like a dog's, but much, much bigger.

An enormous footprint.

A wolf.

◇

It was the first of many footprints found around the village that day. They appeared outside henhouses and barns and sheds and even cottages. A huge wolf had prowled the village that night, and people were afraid. All day the air echoed with the noise of sawing and hammering as doors and walls were patched and strengthened. Meanwhile people went off in little groups, following the path to the edge of the forest. They found pad marks there as well, and they came back hurrying, looking over their shoulders. That evening the village street was quiet and there were no children playing on the green. People were all inside, with shutters closed and locks turned. Polly was inside too, up in her little room, staring out of the window at the great shadowy forest on the edge of the village.

Somewhere in the forest was Diamond.

The world looked very blurry to Polly, thinking that. She had to swallow and rub her eyes, over and over. So it was some time before she noticed the fir cone.

There was a fir cone on her windowsill.

That was an odd place to find a fir cone. The strangeness of it woke Polly up a little, enough to let her go downstairs. Half the village had gathered at the inn, beer was flowing, and the frightening old stories about the forest were being dusted off and polished up and told like they were new.

'What about Granny?' asked Polly, clutching her fir cone as she came forward into the lamplight. 'Did anyone go and see if Granny was safe?'

'Old Granny can look after herself,' said the innkeeper. 'Proper old witch, she is. She'll take no harm.'

'She is NOT an old witch!' exclaimed Polly indignantly. 'She is my friend! She is the kindest person I know!'

'Now then, now then,' said an old man reprovingly. 'Talking like that, when the folk here have taken such care of you! That's not nice, is it? And after they just lost that lovely pig!'

'He was lovely,' agreed Polly, grateful for such kind words about Diamond.

'Ham,' said the old man, nodding, 'and bacon. Pork and crackling too, I daresay.'

'Sausage,' added the innkeeper.

'Black pudding,' sighed his wife.

Then at last Polly understood what the girls had not told her, and what Tom had not mentioned, and also why it was not a good idea to give a name to a pig. Back in her room, looking out towards the forest, she thought, *I'm glad the wolf came. Perhaps Diamond escaped.*

He wouldn't have escaped the innkeeper, but perhaps he escaped the wolf.

◇

In the morning there was more news, and worse. Tom's uncle, the red-faced farmer, was going from farm to farm and cottage to cottage asking, 'Has anybody seen young Tom?'

Tom had vanished, and nobody knew where or when.

The innkeeper thought he knew. He told Tom's uncle, 'I caught sight of him hanging around here. I'll have the price of that pig from you!'

'The price of the pig!' roared Tom's uncle. 'The price of the pig! Were there not wolf prints all around your pigsty? And weren't you the first to cry Wolf! My guess is he went missing in the forest searching for that pig, and I'll have the price of his labour from you!'

The boys Tom's age had another idea. It was that Tom had had enough of working for his uncle and had simply run away. The surprise, the boys said, was that he hadn't done it sooner.

The girls said, 'Poor Tom!' and dabbed their eyes and hunted for frostbitten flowers to make into a wreath. They left it by the oak tree on the green where Tom had often collected acorns for catapult bullets, or climbed in search of caterpillars to drop down their necks, or simply stood boasting with his hands in his pockets. 'We're making it a memorial tree,' they told Polly. 'Aren't you going to help?'

'How can I help?' asked Polly.

'We're each going to tie a hair ribbon to show we'll never forget him.'

'What if he comes back and sees them?' asked Polly. 'He'd never stop laughing. He'd be awful.'

The girls looked at her with reproachful blue eyes, and thought she was hard-hearted.

Most people in the village agreed with Tom's uncle,

that Tom had gone too far into the forest. After much talk, they collected men and dogs for a search party, but they didn't get far.

'They only did it to make themselves feel better,' Polly told Granny. 'Like the girls with their tree.'

'You didn't tie a ribbon then?' asked Granny.

'No,' said Polly, holding her fir cone. 'I think he'll come back.'

◇

Tom didn't come back, and the village changed. Now no one doubted that there were wolves in the forest. Bears too, almost certainly bears, and who knew what besides? A message was sent to the King, far away: 'Send a huntsman!'

There was no reply. Winter closed in. People locked and barred their doors at night, and huddled close to their winter fires. The fields that lay nearest to the forest were left empty. The trees seemed to move closer.

Only Polly, in her red hood and cloak, dared go along the path under the darkness of the ancient branches. She went once a week to visit Granny, and nothing the innkeeper or his wife or anyone else in the village could say would stop her.

'Keep to the path!' the innkeeper's wife warned.

'I do,' said Polly.

'Don't stop to pick flowers, nor nothing like that.'

'There aren't any flowers in winter.'

'Don't go, Polly!' said the girls. 'It's not safe! They say there are bears.'

'Granny says there aren't.'

'Does she say there aren't wolves?'

'I should love to see a wolf!' said Polly.

But all that winter she saw nothing but frosted ferns and black forest tracks and old Granny waving from her cottage door, calling, 'I saw you from away down the path!'

When the first snow fell there was a wonder waiting for Polly at the little house in the forest.

'He come marching up to the door like he'd lived here all his life!' said Granny.

And there was Diamond. Diamond, fat with beech nuts and acorns, and lately with Granny's porridge. Polly got down on her knees to hug the little pig, and her tears of thankfulness rolled down so fast they caused him to snort and sneeze.

'Now what we will do,' said Granny, when the happy reunion had become slightly less damp, 'is build him a little pen round the back of the house where it won't show from the path.'

'Do you mind?' asked Polly anxiously. 'Did you want a pig, Granny?'

'I can't say I did,' said Granny, 'but it seems that I have one. I daresay he will come in useful!'

'And he will be safe,' said Polly thankfully, and she

asked again, 'Are there wolves, Granny?'

But Granny's answer was the same as before. 'There are and there aren't,' she replied.

◇

'One day,' said the villagers, 'that Red Riding Hood will set off into the forest and not come back.'

The villagers said wolves had been heard, howling under a full moon on the edge of the fields. Once again they sent a message to the King.

Polly told Granny, 'The village has sent for a huntsman. That's twice now.'

'Fools,' said Granny.

'Do you hear the howling at night, Granny?'

'I do not,' said Granny. 'I hear owls. What's that in your hand?'

'A white stone,' said Polly, showing her.

'Where did you find it?'

'On a bank of green moss,' said Polly.

'That's a mystery,' said Granny.

'Mmm,' said Polly.

She put the white stone with the fir cone.

◇

Time passed. Late in the spring there was a molehill with a jay's blue wing feather sticking out the top. One summer morning Polly saw a red rose in the duck pond. On the oak tree on the village green, half a dozen faded hair ribbons fluttered under the leaves. When the leaves fell, they were still there. Whole months passed when no one mentioned Tom's name. Polly grew tall, and was now too old to be sent back to the orphanage.

'What were we thinking of?' asked the innkeeper's wife, meaning, *what were we thinking of, taking her in. That cold morning. Gold earrings. We might have known!* She looked crossly towards Polly, who pushed her hair behind her ears so her earrings showed. Polly half fascinated and half alarmed the customers at the inn. She had a way of slamming glasses down that made them jump. It was a rather slamming autumn, what with glasses and doors and Polly's replies to some customers' remarks.

Winter came again, with bitter winds. The cold and the neglected fields made the forest seem more menacing than ever. For the third time, the villagers sent for a huntsman, and this time their message was answered. A huntsman came, a silent fellow in greens and browns and soft leather boots. He carried a gun. The innkeeper admired it very much.

'Double-barrelled,' he said with satisfaction. 'Bang, bang! About time!'

'The poor wolves!' said Polly.

'Wolves are outlaws,' said the innkeeper.

'Outlaws are wolves,' said the huntsman, winking horribly at Polly. 'Got yourself a boyfriend yet?'

'No, have you?' asked Polly, shutting him up.

It seemed a long time since the rose in the pond. The ribbons on the oak tree were shredded to thread, and the path to the pigsty was overgrown with weeds. Polly looked at the huntsman's gun again and, at the first chance she got, she put on her red riding hood cloak and went to see Granny.

'That cloak has got short on you,' said Granny. 'More like a cape.'

'Granny, what's beyond the forest?'

'Hills,' said Granny, 'purple and blue.'

'And over the hills?'

'That's far away, Polly love.'

'Too far to ever come back?'

'Let's hope not,' said Granny.

'There is a huntsman in the forest now,' Polly told her. 'He stopped at the inn, and I saw him. He was sent by the King. He has a gun. The innkeeper says wolves are outlaws.'

'He always was a fool,' said Granny robustly.

'And the huntsman says outlaws are wolves.'

'Shows he knows nothing then,' said Granny. 'I knew many a fine outlaw, back in the days! Stop your worrying, Poll, and go round the back and have a word with Diamond. He'll cheer you up!'

'Has he come in useful yet?' asked Polly.

'Any time now!' said Gran.

◇

Any time now! thought Polly, as she trudged back to the inn that afternoon, and the words made her feel lighter. She remembered them often, as she worked through the days, or shivered herself to sleep at night.

Everyone was cold that winter. Granny tucked up her four hens in together with the two white goats. Diamond, as long as his feet were clean, was allowed into the house to sleep. He slept most of the day, as well as all night, on an old quilt at the end of Granny's bed.

'He'd be in the bed, if I gave him the chance,' said Granny. 'And he snores. But then, so do I. Polly, that fella's about.'

'The huntsman?'

'I've spoken to him. He hangs around here. He says this is the place any wolf would come, with the goats and the hens.'

'And Diamond,' said Polly.

'Well, he never saw the pig. The pig was indoors. Diamond's safe, Polly, but you be careful. He fires that gun at a shadow. You make sure you wear your red cloak. You'll not take him by surprise in that. Or . . .' Granny paused.

'Or what?'

'You could stay safe home.'

'No thank you!' said Polly.

Some nights the frost was so bitter it froze the branches on the trees. They split with sounds louder than gunfire and dropped without warning.

'You want to keep out of that forest, Poll!' warned the innkeeper.

'No I don't,' said Polly.

◇

One morning, towards the end of winter, Polly found a handful of frost feathers in the middle of the forest path. They must have only been there a moment. They were so light a breath of wind would blow them away. Polly stooped and gathered them into her hand and waited as they melted on her mitten.

It was very quiet.

Polly became aware of being watched. Of the way ahead blocked. Of breath, not her own, smoking in the frosty air.

She looked up, and there at last was the wolf.

'And where are you going, Red Riding Hood?' asked the wolf.

Bang, bang, bang, went Polly's heart.

The wolf grinned. White teeth. 'Don't worry. I won't eat you,' he said.

'No you won't!' said Polly, and she tucked her hands under her cloak so that their shaking was hidden, and looked boldly at the wolf. She had never imagined he would be so big. His eyes were the yellow gold of bracken in autumn. He leaned on a tall carved staff. Polly noticed that when he moved it, it left behind the mark of a huge wolf pad. Had this wolf once tried to carry away a little black pig?

'All alone, Red Riding Hood,' the wolf said mockingly. 'Aren't you frightened?'

'No I'm not,' said Polly, 'but you should be.'

'Why should I be?'

'There's a huntsman in the forest,' Polly said. 'He says wolves are outlaws, and outlaws are wolves. He has a gun. He hangs around Granny's house, watching out for you. You should go away! You should go far away, over the hills!'

'I'd rather come with you,' said the wolf.

'Well, you can't,' said Polly, and pushed past him and ran, bright in her red cloak, calling, 'Granny! Granny! Granny!' so that the huntsman stepped back into the shadows.

Granny's door was open, despite the cold. 'Come in, Polly!' she called. 'I knew you'd be along. I'm in bed.'

'In bed?' repeated Polly, astonished.

'I had a tumble. I'm resting my foot,' explained Granny, as Polly came panting into the cottage. 'I should never have tried to climb on the roof . . .'

'On the roof!'

'That's no matter just now. Are you all right, Polly? You look bothered. Come close!'

'Granny . . .'

Granny raised a finger to her lips and nodded towards the door. 'That hunter's about!' she whispered. 'Did you see him?'

'No! Where?

'Around in the shadows. Listening, I daresay. Talk natural!'

Polly nodded.

'I knew you'd be worried, finding me in bed,' said Granny, in a loud, clear voice. 'Polly, what big eyes you've got!'

'All the better for watching where I'm going,' said Polly. 'There were frost feathers on the path, Granny!'

Polly gazed at Granny, willing her to understand.

'Were there now?' said Granny. 'After all this time! I should like to have seen them. Nearby?'

Polly nodded, looking at the open door.

'Dear, dear,' said Granny, briskly. 'Cold enough for frost feathers and the fire out and that poor soul outside under the eaves looking out for wolves and whatever . . .'

'Outlaws!' growled the huntsman's voice, sounding terribly, terribly close.

'Wonderful hearing these huntsmen do have!' said Granny, glancing at Polly from under the large lace nightcap she wore. 'Never misses a word! Tell him to come in out of the wind, Polly love!'

Polly went out with the message, but the huntsman would not come in. Nor would he let Polly leave again. 'You stay with the old woman!' he ordered. 'There's something about!'

'I came through the forest,' said Polly, speaking much more loudly than she needed to do. 'You don't need your GUN! I didn't see anything to worry about!'

'You keep your voice down, miss, and get inside!' said the huntsman.

'Why? What are you frightened of?' demanded Polly, twirling around in her red cloak, as if trying to see. 'What made you think THERE WAS SOMETHING ABOUT?'

'I'll not stand for this!' exploded the huntsman, and he actually marched Polly back to the house and sat her down in the rocking chair. 'There!' he said. 'So long as I hear that chair rock and those bed springs creak, I shall know where you are!' And he stormed back outside.

'Oh Granny!' exclaimed Polly, frightened and furious. 'Whatever . . .' Just in time she remembered the open door. 'Whatever were you doing on the roof?'

'That chimney pot is loose,' said Granny. 'And I hopped up to try to fix it before it came down all together. Slipped off and twisted my ankle, which is why I'm here in bed. 'Tis dangerous, a loose chimney pot.'

Polly's eyes became suddenly bright.

'It might slip and roll down on anyone,' said Granny.

Polly didn't reply. She was thinking so hard that she was perfectly still, and she jumped when the huntsman poked his head round the door.

'Gone quiet!' he said, glancing at Granny under her lace cap, and Polly's red cloak. 'Just checking!'

'Stay for a bit and get warm,' said Granny, but he was gone again in a moment. Diamond, dozing, stirred in his sleep, and suddenly Polly knew what to do. There was the window beside Granny's bed, with the pen they had built for Diamond outside. If she climbed on the pen she could reach the roof. From the top of the roof she could see down the path . . .

Polly rocked the rocking chair, *bump, rock, bump*, with her eyes on Granny's. Granny turned and creaked in bed, her eyes on Polly's. Polly looked down at

Diamond, and began undoing the ribbons of her cloak. 'I hope your foot doesn't hurt too much when you move,' she said politely and clearly to Granny, and she did not forget to rock.

'I daresay I will manage,' replied Granny, and she did not forget to creak.

'I suppose it is nearly TIME FOR BED,' said Polly, and she lifted the sleeping Diamond, who had learned those words long before, when he was a slim black piglet in the garden of the inn.

Often Granny had said that Diamond would one day come in useful. Now the time had come at last. The next time the huntsman looked into the door, there was someone in the bed, wriggling and creaking, with their lace nightcap pulled down to their nose. And there was someone in a red cloak, rocking in the rocking chair.

But Polly was on the roof.

Creak! went Granny's bed. Polly could hear it in the room beneath.

Bump! went the rocking chair.

Grunt, grunt, grunt! went the person in the nightcap. And Granny said, clear and bright, 'Oh Polly, what a shocking cold you've got. I never heard such a cough!'

Polly had a clear view of the forest path. Beside her was the chimney pot. She could watch for the wolf, and if the worst came to the worst, the huntsman was standing under the eaves, and the chimney pot was loose . . .

'You need to rub your chest with rum and oil!' continued Granny, rocking. Diamond gave a sudden startled squeal and Granny told him not to be foolish. Polly could not see the huntsman, but looking over the ridge pole she could see his shadow on the frosty grass. Then, far down the forest path amongst the frosty flickering shadows, she saw a movement.

Suddenly many things happened at once.

The wolf stepped out from the trees.

The shadow of the huntsman raised the shadow of a gun.

Polly lifted the chimney pot, and in the house Granny heard her do it.

'Polly, take care!' she cried, but too late.

Crash! went the chimney pot, as it rolled off the roof.

Bang! went the gun, shooting wildly into the air.

Wallop! went the huntsman, falling to the ground.

'Tom! Tom!' cried Polly, rolling, and bowling and tumbling off the roof, and Tom ran and caught her as she fell.

'Diamond!' called Granny, as Diamond heard the excitement and leaped from the bed. 'Diamond, come back with my nightcap!'

◇

This is the story of how Red Riding Hood saved the wolf, Tom, with the help of Granny and the cooperation of Diamond the pig.

It is also the story of how Tom Piper stole the pig Diamond from the innkeeper and his wife, and ran away to seek his fortune in the land of over the hills and far away. Tom reached that land (although Diamond escaped on the journey) but returned to the forest from time to time. Far away can be too far away, when the wrong people are left behind.

As well, it is the story of how Diamond the pig came to be useful at last.

It isn't the story, because it has ended too soon, of how Granny returned the huntsman to the village in her wheelbarrow, and went back to her happy life in the forest as a semi-retired smuggler, with Diamond for company.

Nor is it the ridiculous mixed-up tale told by the huntsman of a wolf in bed, and Granny eaten, and Red Riding Hood saved by his own brave self, rushing in with an axe.

'Where did you get an axe from?' the villagers asked him. 'And where is the dead wolf, not to mention Red Riding Hood? And how did Granny come alive again? You had a knock on the head with a chimney pot, and plainly you're not over it yet!'

◇

Tom returned over the hills and Polly went with him. When they married, Granny came to the wedding and so did Diamond. Diamond wore a scarlet waistcoat and carried a basket of primroses in his teeth, proving for a second time that pigs have other uses besides bacon, ham and sausage. After the wedding Polly and Tom lived excitingly ever after, in a town beside the sea, backed by blue and purple hills. It never felt far away to Polly and Tom. Quite the opposite: it felt exactly like home.

8

Things Were Different in Those Days

or

The Twelve Dancing Princesses

By the time that Violet was nine years old, there were only three people left at home in the palace. These were Violet, and her mother, and her grandfather, the Old King. However, there were also the lodgers who came and went, bothering Violet, exhausting the Queen, and causing great grumbles from the Old King whenever he happened to notice them. This was not often, because the Old King was ancient. He sat for whole days and nights in his shadowy corner of the kitchen, muttering, dozing, and banging with his stick.

'In his own world,' said Violet's mother, the Queen.

Sometimes, though, he would say things to show he

was partly in their world too. For instance, when there was trouble with a lodger not paying his bill, or stealing the candlesticks, or announcing that he was vegetarian when it was sausages and bacon for supper – then the Old King would rouse from his dozing and become *very* noisy.

'Off with their noddles! Off with their noddles!' he would shout. 'It saved a great deal of trouble in my day!'

'But what,' demanded Violet, when she was old enough to pay attention to her grandfather's remarks, 'is a noddle?'

'Nothing, nothing, take no notice,' said her mother, irritably scrambling eggs for vegetarians. 'Stop sucking that honey spoon! DON'T put it back in the pot! Dry those plates if you want to help!'

Violet, who never wanted to help, retreated back to her grandfather's corner.

'Yer noddle,' he said, jabbing at her with his stick, 'is yer head!'

'What!' exclaimed Violet. 'You didn't really!'

'I did an' all,' said the Old King. 'I offed many a noddle in the good old days!'

'Violet, stop encouraging him!' snapped the Queen, scraping black bits off the toast while the eggs turned leathery and the sausages began to smoke. 'Things were different in those days! Oh, WHERE is the butter?'

'I gave it to the cat,' said Violet.

'Violet!'

'It was licking it anyway. It had got it all hairy.'

'I don't know why I bother,' moaned her mother, piling her terrible cooking on to a battered golden tray.

'Why *do* you bother?' asked Violet.

'I'm saving up,' said her mother.

'What for?'

'It's about time you learned to do something useful. Get the door for me, do, and take those shoes off the table. I was giving them a polish, but there's no time now. You might give them a rub if the cat's left any butter. Otherwise I'll do them with marge when I get back.'

The cat, however, had not left any butter, and Violet skipped off quickly while her mother was out of the kitchen, not wanting to be about when the washing up began. Violet did not care for washing up, nor cooking breakfasts or polishing shoes.

She spent her days in other ways.

Prancing along the dusty empty corridors in ancient satin dresses.

Twirling with her arms outstretched in front of misty mirrors.

Searching in the garden for long-lost buried treasure.

Drawing with charcoal on old palace portraits, spectacles on the gentlemen and moustaches on the ladies.

Climbing about on the roof tiles, attempting to catch pigeons.

Roasting slices of apple over candle flames.

Making perfume from squashed rose petals in empty honey pots. This was something Violet could never get quite right. Her perfume always smelt wonderful for one day, peculiar for two days, and then dreadful ever after, as well as turning green. When it reached the green-and-dreadful stage, Violet said, 'Witch's soup,' and poured it into the moat.

When Violet wasn't doing any of these things, she either hung around the kitchen, saying she was bored, or else she went exploring in the ancient palace. She peered through the keyholes of long-locked doors, and she hunted through musty cupboards that had been closed for years.

The most interesting thing Violet saw through the keyholes was a room with twelve beds.

'Hmm,' said her mother when Violet described this discovery. 'Take your grandfather this cup of tea and mop his chin after!'

The most interesting thing Violet found in the cupboards was twelve musical boxes.

◇

Twelve musical boxes, and they all played different tunes. Violet found if she wound them quickly, she could set them all going at once. Then 'Oranges and Lemons' mixed with 'Ring a Ring o' Roses'; and 'Cherry Ripe' with 'The Muffin Man'; and 'Over the Hills and Far Away' with 'Jack Be Nimble' – and all the other tunes ('Hey Diddle Diddle', 'Green Grow the Rushes, O', 'Scottish Bluebells', 'Goosey Goosey Gander', 'Little Bo Beep' and 'Mary, Mary, Quite Contrary') jangled together too, so it sounded like a room full of mad, plinking, silvery starlings.

Violet played this winding-up game for a long time before looking at the boxes themselves. When she did, she saw that each one was carved with a letter on the lid:

A, B, C, D, E, F, G, H, I, J, K, L

Violet traced the letters with her forefinger. It came away grey with dust.

Then, with some difficulty, Violet piled up all twelve musical boxes in her arms and staggered with them to the kitchen. There she laid them out on the kitchen table and wound them up to play. Her mother was upstairs, making beds and sweeping, but the Old King, her grandfather, was nod, nod, nodding in his chair. The sound of the boxes woke him, or half woke him. When the last tune had wound down into silence, he suddenly spoke:

'Anastasia, Bella, Cordelia, Della
        Eglantine
            Florentine
                Geraldine
                    Harriet, Imogen, Jessica,
                    Kate . . .'

Violet stared at him in astonishment. 'And last of all,
Grandfather?' she prompted.

'Anastasia, Bella, Cordelia, Della
     Eglantine
          Florentine
               Geraldine
                    Harriet, Imogen, Jessica,
                    Kate – and last of all?'

'Lilian,' murmured her Grandfather. 'Last of all, Lilian, long, long ago, when I offed with their princes' noddles!'

'You offed with their princes' noddles?' repeated Violet.

'Aye,' said her grandfather, sleepily.

'Tell me more!' ordered Violet. 'Tell me more, you awful old man!' And she joggled his elbow, and shook his chair, but it did no good. He ignored her completely and wound down into silence, like one of the music boxes. Nothing could wake him; not cold water dripped down his neck, nor toast crusts scorched under his nose. Violet was forced to wait until her mother staggered in with a huge pile of ironing before she could learn any more.

◊

'There!' said her mother with a sigh, dumping the ironing on the dresser and collapsing on to a stool. 'Ten sheets, ten pillowcases, five counterpanes. All to be ironed by bedtime.'

'Don't do it!' said Violet.

'I have to do it. Lodgers like it.'

'Why do they like it?'

'Makes them looked washed.'

'They are washed, aren't they?'

'Now and then,' said the Queen. 'Take your grubby hands off; you'll make them even worse. Whatever is all that clutter on the table?'

'Come and see!' said Violet.

So her mother heaved herself up from her stool and went over to the table and then, 'Oh!' she said. 'Oh!'

'Music boxes,' said Violet.

Her mother nodded and picked up the one with the 'A' on the lid, and wound it up. The tune was 'Green Grow the Rushes, O', and when it got to the sad end, *One is one and all alone and ever more shall be so*, a tear rolled down her cheek, a real tear, the first tear Violet had ever seen her cry.

It had an astonishing effect on Violet. It made her rush to her mother and hug her tight and say, 'You're not all alone! You've got me!'

'Course I have,' said her mother. 'Takes me back, that's all.' And she wound the music box with the 'L' on the lid and it played 'Mary, Mary, Quite Contrary', and from the old rocking chair in the shadowy corner an ancient voice, a cracked, wicked, wheezy, old, old voice joined in the song.

'*An' pretty maids all in a row!*' sang the Old King, Violet's grandfather. 'Twelve!'

'Twelve,' repeated Violet.

'Twelve Princesses! Twelve Dancing Princesses! Well, eleven and our Annie!'

Suddenly Violet understood, and recited:

> *'Anastasia, Bella, Cordelia, Della*
> > *Eglantine*
> > > *Florentine*
> > > > *Geraldine*
> > > > > *Harriet, Imogen, Jessica,*
> > > > > *Kate – and last of all, Lilian*
> > > > > ... They were the twelve
> > > > > dancing princesses!'

'It's true, they were,' said her mother.

'And you were one of them?'

'I was.'

'And they were your sisters? And these were their musical boxes?'

'You were bound to know sometime.'

'And you were the first!' Violet continued, looking at her mother. 'Anastasia!'

'They called me Plain Annie,' said her mother.

'Did they?'

'Well, I was plain. Compared.'

'How could you have been, when you are beautiful now?'

Her mother looked at her red, worn, lumpy-with-washing hands, and then tucked a strand of wispy hair behind her ear and said, 'Oh Violet! How you remind me of our little Lil!'

'You mean Lilian? Last-of-all Lilian?'

'That's right.'

'Was she pretty?'

'No prettier than you.'

'Was she clever?'

'She might have been.'

'Where is she now?'

'I must get on with this ironing.'

'Why must you get on with the ironing?'

'Because I'm saving up!' said her mother.

◇

Violet fiddled with the music boxes for some time more. Then she got under the table and tried to make the cat dance, rolled herself in the hearth rug, unrolled again, wrote VIOLET in the dust on the dresser, and got in the way of the iron.

'I'm bored,' she said.

'That's because you don't know anything useful.'

'What's useful?

'All sorts. Things you learn in books, numbers and figures and the names of the stars. They're useful. If you could build a bridge, that's useful. If you could draw a map, that's useful.'

'Girls can't do things like that!' objected Violet.

'They could, if they learned.'

'Could you?'

'I never learned. Take a comb to your grandfather's whiskers, Violet; they've got all draggley again.'

'No thank you. They've got bits in! Do you know what he told me about the princesses?'

'What did he tell you?'

'That he offed with their princes' noddles!'

'Ah.'

'Did he really? Is it true? What happened to them all after that?'

'You've got to remember, things were different in those days,' said her mother, spitting on the iron to see if it was hot. 'You've got to remember that, if I tell you!'

'I will, I will!'

'And . . .' Violet's mother paused.

'Yes, yes?' said Violet impatiently.

'There was a lot more magic about.'

'Was there?'

'Folk took it for granted,' said her mother. 'Foolish, I call it. Anyway, there was us twelve princesses and our mother dead after Lilian was born and our father with his ways . . .'

'Off with their noddles,' murmured Violet's grandfather from his corner. 'Them were the good old days.'

Violet's mother looked across at him thoughtfully.

'He's dribbling on the cat again,' she said. 'Fetch it off his lap, Violet!'

'The cat doesn't mind,' said Violet.

'I mind,' said her mother, and put down her iron and shooed the cat away. 'Well, there was us twelve girls, and me expected to keep charge. And that wasn't easy, especially come night.'

'Why come night?'

'They liked dancing,' said Violet's mother. 'They liked dancing and prancing and twirls and curls and curtsying and silk and lace.'

'What else?' asked Violet.

'Gems and jewels and sparkly things. Perfumes and powders and rouges and ribbons. Waltzes, polkas and polonaises. And princes for partners. And most of all, they liked satin dancing shoes.'

'Well, didn't you too?' asked Violet.

'I did,' admitted her mother. 'Though I was the plain one.'

'Satin dancing shoes!' murmured Violet, looking down at her own shabby boots.

'They wore out them shoes!' growled the Old King suddenly. 'Twelve pair a night! Twelve pair a night in rags and holes and I didn't LIKE it!'

◇

'Your grandfather and those dancing shoes!' said Violet's

mother. 'He fussed and he grumbled and he said, "How'd you girls wear out twelve pair of them shoes?" Because, you see, Violet, we weren't allowed out after nightfall. It was straight off to bed and the door locked behind us.'

'I found your bedroom!' said Violet. 'I saw through the keyhole! Twelve beds in one room and no space to dance! So how DID you wear out your shoes?'

'Ah,' said her mother, 'that's what he wanted to know. And he set about to find out. He put out an announcement: any prince who could discover how the princesses wore their satin shoes to rags and holes could choose his princess and take over the rule of the kingdom! "Because I've had enough of it," said he. Three nights each he gave for the task. Three nights for each prince to find out.'

'And if they couldn't?' asked Violet.

'Then off with their noddles!' wheezed her grandfather from his corner. 'With my little noddle-offer!'

'Grandfather!' exclaimed Violet. 'You never had a noddle-offer! Did you? Did you?'

'I did an' all,' said her grandfather happily.

'Where is it now?'

'Never you mind!' snapped her mother. 'Never you mind where it is now. A nasty thing like that!'

'Well then, what about the princes?' demanded Violet. 'Did lots of princes come?'

'Of course they did,' said her mother. 'There was no

shortage of princes. If ever there were pretty maids all in a row, it was my eleven sisters! The princes came, and one by one they were put to bed in our room, with scented sheets and white down pillows, with honey cakes to eat and hot spiced wine to drink. And their eyes would close and next thing they knew it would be bright morning and twelve more pairs of dancing shoes in rags and holes!'

'And what did Grandfather do then?'

'Oh, he went shouting about the castle about the cost of satin shoes and the uselessness of princes, and the first prince would be gone, then the second, then the third . . .'

Violet's mother paused her ironing and sighed.

'Well . . .' she said, and sighed again.

'Off with their noddles?' whispered Violet.

Her mother nodded.

'AWFUL Grandfather!'

'I told you, things were different in those days, but even so, such a to-do, the first time it happened! That was Bella's prince.'

'Oh no!'

'Oh yes! She cried all day until bedtime.'

'Then what?'

'Then on with her dancing shoes!'

'Not truly!'

'They *did* do things different in those days,' her

mother reminded her. 'And there was a *lot* more magic about. Not that you should ever rely on magic, Violet! Common sense and hard work are what I've always banked on.'

'And lodgers,' said Violet.

'That's because I'm saving up. *Don't* sit on those ironed sheets and *don't* eat jam with your fingers!'

Violet wiped her fingers on a pillowcase and asked, 'What happened after Bella's prince had his noddle noddled off?'

'Cordelia's tried next. Then Della's. Eglantine, Florentine, Geraldine (they were triplets), their princes came next.'

'All noddled off?' asked Violet, wide-eyed.

Her mother nodded. 'And after them, Harriet's and Imogen's and Jessica's and Kate's, and last of all Lilian's.'

'Did Lilian go dancing the day her prince's noddle was noddled off?'

'She couldn't wait!'

'Well!' said Violet. 'I think that's awful! All those poor princes and wicked old Grandfather! Why do we still keep him?'

'You can't go getting rid of people just like that!'

'*He* did!'

'Yes, but things were different in those days.'

There was a pause then, and a hot scorching smell,

while another sheet was ironed. Violet frowned in thought, trying to understand.

'Did you have a prince?' she asked at last. 'What about Father? When did he come into the story?'

'Too many questions,' said her mother. 'First I have to tell you about the soldier.'

'What soldier?'

'Back from the wars.'

'What wars?'

'And travelling the country, looking for work.'

'What sort of work?'

'Any sort of work because he hadn't any money.'

'Don't soldiers get paid?'

'If they do, they spend it. They can't hold on to money. It's not in their natures . . .' Violet's mother held a pillowcase, worn thin as tissue paper, up to the light. 'It'll drop to bits if I wash it,' she said.

'Throw it away and buy another!'

'I can't. I'm saving up.'

◇

'Anyway,' said Violet, interrupting the ironing once more. 'You haven't finished the story at all! What about the soldier?'

'He came long after the last of the princes, although not before the last of the dancing. He would never have come, but he met an old woman on the road. An old woman, bent under a burden of firewood and kindling.

He offered to carry it and she let him. And when the wood was set down at the old woman's house she thanked him and asked him his plans.

"'I'm out to seek my fortune," said he.

"'There's a fortune at the palace," the old woman said, "for anyone that can solve a mystery." Then she told him the tale of the twelve dancing princesses and the shoes worn to rags and holes by morning, and the King offering a princess and the rule of the country to anyone who could tell him how it happened. And the soldier said, "That'll do me!"

"'Well," said the old woman, "you helped me, and now I'll help you. So listen! When you reach the palace and you're shut in for the night, in the princesses' bedroom . . . if they let you try . . . if you dare . . ."

"'They'll let me," said the soldier. "I've a way with words. And of course I dare. What have I got to lose?"

"'Your noddle," said the old woman.

"'It'll not come to that," said the soldier.

"'Not if you do as I tell you," said the old woman. "Now remember this! Eat nothing, drink nothing, and wear the gift I give you!"

'And then the old woman took from a chest a thin, grey cloak and she gave it to the soldier because he'd carried the firewood home.'

'And that night did the soldier get locked in the room with you and the other princesses?' asked Violet.

'He did.'

'And did you give him honey cakes, like each time before?'

'We did, but we found out afterwards that he hid them all under his hat.'

'But you gave him hot spiced wine?'

'We did, but we found out afterwards that he poured it away into his boots.'

'And then what?'

'And then he lay back on his white down pillows and closed his eyes. Solid as a tree trunk and snoring like a porker and he never moved nor blinked, even when we poked him. Fast asleep, we thought. So then . . .'

'What? What?'

'Off with our nightgowns, and on with the silks and taffetas! Velvet and damask and lace like foam! Buttoned gloves, coral beads, pearl rings, diamond bracelets! Perfumes, powders, gilt tiaras and satin dancing shoes!'

'And then?'

'We piled on to the middle bed, all of us in a heap . . . and then, *Whoosh!*'

'*Whoosh?*'

'Down through the floor it sank . . .'

'The *bed* sank?'

Her mother nodded.

'And in a moment, less than a moment, we had reached the avenues of silver trees and golden trees and diamond trees that led down to the lakeside.'

'All *that* was under the bed?'

'It was. A whole glittering kingdom!'

'Every night?'

'That's right. There was a lot more magic about in those days, don't forget!'

'And nobody knew about it all except you?'

'Nobody knew about it but me and my sisters. Not till that night.'

'Oh!' said Violet. 'I'd forgotten the soldier!'

'I hadn't!' said her mother. 'Not then. Not ever. Anyway . . .'

'*Whoosh!* went the bed,' prompted Violet, 'and down you all went to the avenues of silver and gold and diamond trees!'

'Yes, and we set off, just as we did every night, under the silver trees, and Lilian said suddenly, "What was that?"

'"What was what?" I asked.

'"I heard a leaf plucked," said Lilian. "Right behind me!"

'Lilian was always a girl to jump at shadows, and there was nothing behind her – we looked. So on we went, hurrying. And under the golden trees Lilian started again, "What was that?"

'"What was what?" we asked her.

'"I heard a flower picked," she said. "Right behind me!"

'But there was nothing and we told her so, and we left the golden trees behind us, and there was the diamond avenue leading down to the water, every leaf and branch shining, and Lilian stopped and spun around.

'"I heard a twig snapped!" said she. "Right behind me!"

'Well, we hadn't heard it, but to please her we looked along the avenues and amongst the trees and we couldn't see anything but sparkles and shadows.

'"Someone is following us, I'm sure they are!" said Lilian, clutching my hand.

'It was just then that I heard a swish, like a cloak might swish, and I thought perhaps she was right. But still there was no one to be seen and the others were hurrying down to the lakeside, and so we hurried too. We could see the boats by then.'

'What boats?' asked Violet.

'The twelve little boats like seashells that waited by the lakeside to carry us over the water.'

'Over the water to where?'

'To the castle in the middle where the dancing was. Even from the lakeside you could hear the violins and trumpets and the flutes and drums. And there were rockets whizzing up and reflecting on the water and a warm smell of spices and perfumes and lilies, but that wasn't why my sisters started running.'

'Why did they, then?'

'Because in each of those boats, except the one at the end, sat a prince!'

'Not the noddled-off princes?' exclaimed Violet.

'The very same! With not a hair harmed. Waving and smiling and nodding their heads, and waiting to row them across to the palace, just as they did every night!'

'Oh, how wonderful!' said Violet.

'I told you,' said her mother, smiling over the ironing, 'there was a lot more magic in those days!'

'But . . .' began Violet. 'But . . .' she said, hastily choosing from a hundred questions. 'But Mother, who rowed you?'

'I rowed myself,' said her mother. 'But Violet, my boat weighed extra heavy that night!'

'Did it?'

'Yes.'

'And when you reached the island, did you dance all night?'

'We did.'

'And then you went home?'

'That's right.'

'How?'

'Same way as we got there.'

'And the soldier?' asked Violet. 'What happened to the soldier?'

'He was fast asleep when we got back! Fast asleep and snoring, with his cloak hanging over the end

of his bed, all wet about the hem.'

'All wet about the hem?'

'As if it had trailed in water.'

'Had it?'

'Ah!'

'And was Grandfather angry in the morning?'

'Raging. But still we went again the next night.'

'Leaving the soldier snoring, just like before?'

'Just like before.'

'And Lilian?' wondered Violet.

'Yes, Lilian! She heard footsteps under the trees, she said.'

'But nobody was there?'

'Weren't they? The princes were there. And that night, when I climbed into my boat, a voice said, "Leave the oars and close your eyes!" And we shot across the water to the castle!'

'I think it was the soldier!' said Violet. 'I'm sure it was the soldier, but why couldn't you see him?'

'I could dance with him,' said her mother.

'Did you? Did you?'

'Till my shoes wore out.'

'And then when you came back,' prompted Violet, 'where was the soldier? Still asleep in bed?'

'That's right.'

'And his cloak hung over the end?'

'It was.'

'Wet around the hem, as if it had dangled in water?'

'Clever girl,' said Violet's mother. 'And it was the same the next night too, and that was the third night, and by then we knew each other very well, and he'd shown me the secret of the cloak that the old woman gave him for carrying the wood.'

'What secret?'

'When he took it off, there he was!'

'Yes?'

'And when he put it on, there he wasn't!'

'A magic cloak, which made him invisible?'

'Well done!'

'But what happened with Grandfather in the morning?'

'Grandfather in the morning said, "Three nights running! And each night twelve pairs of satin shoes, worn to rags and holes!"

'"Satin doesn't wear well," said the soldier, grinning.

'"Neither does my temper!" your grandfather roared at him. "And now it's off with your noddle!"'

◇

'"It is not off with my noddle," said the soldier to your grandfather, "because I've found out what happens to them satin shoes!" Then he took from his pocket a silver leaf and a golden flower and a twig all set with diamonds, and he told your grandfather the story I've just told you.'

231

'I bet he was surprised!' said Violet.

'He was so surprised he stopped roaring and raging, and he said, "Well lad, choose your princess!"

'"I already did," said the soldier.'

'And it was you?' asked Violet.

'And it was me.'

'And he was Father?'

'Yes he was.'

'And so then you lived happily ever after?'

'Happily,' said her mother, 'but not ever after.'

Then, except for the thump of the iron and the rustle of the sheets, the kitchen was quiet for a while.

'Oh,' said Violet, and she gave a great sigh.

Her mother folded the last of the sheets. The cat rolled over in front of the fire. The Old King opened his eyes.

'I miss my old noddle-offer,' he murmured, and fell back asleep again.

'He's a shocker,' said the Queen, Violet's mother. 'But we'll not change him now. I'd best get back to the bedrooms.'

'Not yet! Not yet! Not yet!' cried Violet, running after her as she left the kitchen. 'I need to ask you things.'

'You'd better come help with the beds, then!'

'Making beds is boring,' grumbled Violet. 'I don't know why we do it.'

'I told you, we're saving up!'

'Should we sell the music boxes?'

'No, we shouldn't.'

'Could we sell the noddle-offer?'

'No, we couldn't.'

'Why not?'

'Well for one thing,' said her mother, 'I dropped it in the moat the day I met your father.'

'You should have dropped it before,' said Violet.

'I should, but I never thought of it, I was that busy running after my sisters.'

'What happened to them after the silver leaf and the golden flower and the twig all set with diamonds?'

'They vanished.'

'Where to?'

'Where do you think?'

'Back to their princes,' said Violet, 'and the shining trees, and the little boats like seashells and the dancing in the castle.'

'I often think,' said her mother, 'that they'll be dancing barefoot by now.'

'They won't care,' said Violet, kicking off her boots and twirling, barefoot herself, not helping at all. 'Oh what lovely times you had! I wish that it was me! Why is the room with the twelve beds kept locked? What happened to Father's magic cloak? Do you think we could fish the noddle-offer out of the moat?'

'Violet!'

'Just for fun!'

'Fun?!'

'I do get bored.'

Her mother had been sweeping dust into piles under the lodgers' beds. Now she stopped and looked at Violet. She looked at her for a long time, very thoughtfully, and she said, 'You'd like that cloak, wouldn't you?'

'Yes I would!'

'You'd fish out the noddle-offer?'

'If I could.'

'You'd be on to that middle bed and off down the avenues and over the lake to that enchanted castle?'

'I'd LOVE to!' said Violet, still twirling.

'And lost like the others,' said her mother. 'Well. It's a good thing I saved up.'

◇

Soon after this, things changed for Violet and her mother and grandfather, and even the cat. They exchanged the castle for a very small house in the city. Violet was sent to a school with navy blue uniforms, lots of homework, and hockey on Saturday mornings. There she learned to do a hundred things she'd always supposed girls couldn't do, and her mother had always supposed they could, if only they had a chance. Once she got used to it, she enjoyed it very much and was never ever bored. The Old King, her grandfather, went to live in a home for tired old men, where he had porridge every morning and cake and ham at teatime and lots of things to grumble about and nurses to wipe his chin.

Violet used to visit him on Saturday afternoons.

'The cat is getting fatter and Mother is much happier,' said Violet, telling him the news. 'She doesn't have to work so hard now we haven't any lodgers.'

'Did you off with their noddles?' asked her grandfather.

'No of course we didn't!' said Violet.

'I'd have offed them,' said her grandfather, his voice quavering with sadness and regret. 'I'd have offed them with my little noddle-offer.'

'I know you would,' said Violet, patting his trembling hands.

'I'm not paying for any more of them satin shoes, if that's what you've come to ask for.'

'I haven't come to ask for anything,' said Violet, all at once sorry for her wicked old grandfather, still worrying his ancient worries. 'I don't wear satin shoes. Me and my friends wear hockey boots.' And she stuck a foot out to show him.

''Ockey!' he murmured, and dozed for a bit

while Violet sat quietly, thinking.

'There wasn't no 'ockey when I was King!' he said, suddenly awake again.

'Poor Grandfather,' said Violet. 'Poor Old King!'

'Poor old king,' he agreed. 'Poor old noddle-offer. Poor lost pretty maids all in a row.'

Violet nodded.

'Poor princes,' he said, and bowed his head.

'Yes,' said Violet gently. 'Poor princes. But Grandfather, things were different in those days. And don't forget,' she added, as she mopped his tumbling tears, 'there was a lot more magic about!'

9

What I Did in the Holidays and Why Hansel's Jacket Is So Tight (by Gretel, aged 10)

or
Hansel and Gretel

Her name was Fraulein Angelika Maria and none of the children could say it. She was twenty years old, and everything about her, from her sea-green shoes (they had gold heels and gold linings) to her astonishing hair (it was dark red and wildly, expensively, shockingly short) looked entirely wrong for a one-roomed school house in the middle of a forest. It was not a nice school house. Fraulein Angelika Maria had never dreamed of such smothering, stifling dullness as she had found in that classroom. It was like a heavy blanket over her head.

However, that was where she was, and this was

the third day of the term. Before she arrived she had planned to stay for a year.

But I didn't *sign* anything, thought Fraulein Angelika Maria with deep, deep relief.

It was a very long way from the city.

Fraulein Angelika Maria and her class of children were halfway through their morning. They had sung a song about all things that were bright and beautiful (or at least Fraulein Angelika Maria had sung it while the children watched in baffled amazement). They had endured a story about a tortoise and a hare. They had been hauled from their desks to stretch their arms, touch their toes, and hop from foot to foot. They were patient children, and so although they looked at each other in bewilderment, they had obediently hopped. And then at last the morning had settled down into a more familiar pattern. Fraulein Angelika Maria was marking the essays that her class had written the day before. The children were toiling through arithmetic.

'Ask me if you need help,' she had told them. 'Don't sit and struggle.'

But they were sitting and struggling.

The schoolroom was heated by a smouldering iron stove. It smelt of damp wood, damp clothes and damp children. Fraulein Angelika wore a delicious perfume named Parisian White Morning, but its smell was not as strong as the schoolroom's, and so it was soon overpowered. The sounds were of hammering rain, heavy breathing, the creak of wooden seats, the rattle and tick of the schoolroom clock, and sniffing. The sniffing and the rain were the loudest. Also there was a drip from the roof.

The problem of drips from the roof had never happened to Fraulein Angelika Maria before. She wondered how to deal with it. The sensible way, she supposed, would be to climb up and locate the hole. The polite way would be to ignore it. Neither seemed possible.

Luckily, the children were used to leaky roofs.

'Shall I get the bucket, miss?' asked a boy.

'Yes please,' said Fraulein Angelika Maria gratefully.

And when the battered enamel bucket was in place, and the dripping had become a loud *plink, plink, plink*, another boy asked, 'Miss, do you want the rag in?'

'The rag?' Fraulein Angelika Maria looked around the room. She had heard of rags, but never actually seen one.

'It's on the rag nail, miss,' said a girl, and there it was, grey and hideous, hung in a corner at the back of the room.

'Certainly not!' said Fraulein Angelika Maria, looking at it in disgust. And she picked it up with the schoolroom poker, carried it across to the stove, lifted the lid, and dropped it in. The room immediately smelt a little better, and Fraulein Angelika Maria felt a little better too, as if a corner of the blanket had lifted. From her beaded green-and-gold silk bag she took a folded linen handkerchief, snow white with her initials in the corner. When it was folded into the bottom of the bucket, the loud *plink, plink, plink* became a much quieter *bump, bump, bump.*

'Wonderful,' Fraulein Angelika Maria said. 'Thank you, everyone, for your help. However, I must ask you all not to call me "miss". "Miss" is not my name, so I find to be called it so often quite *mys*tifying!'

This rather good joke (she thought) drifted brief as a bubble into the schoolroom air, lost its brightness and vanished without a single person noticing it had ever existed. Fraulein Angelika Maria went a little pink about her cheekbones. Nobody noticed that either. They simply sat, waiting for her to say something that they could understand. They did not fidget. They looked ready to sit and wait all day.

'Well,' she said, attempting to sound brisk. 'Well, anyway, my name is Fraulein Angelika Maria, and that is what I would like you to call me.'

There was a slight shuffling on the middle benches, as if they were preparing to bargain.

'Fraulein Angelika Maria,' she repeated. 'But . . .' she glanced at the middle benches, 'Fraulein Angelika will do.'

Class of Fraulein Angelika Maria

The shuffling stopped, but nothing else happened. The children gazed at her with exactly the same expression as they gazed at the raindrops on the windowpanes. Bored, waiting for it to stop. 'The children will be adorable,' her friends in the city had said hopefully, when they had failed to talk her out of her extremely bad idea (which had seemed an extremely good idea at the time) of the school in the middle of the forest.

'Of course they will!' Fraulein Angelika had replied, because she really thought they would be. She had read about country children in fairy tales. They had all been adorable. 'Cherubs!' she had said.

But these children were not cherubs, nor adorable. They were sticky. Their faces and hands, their wooden desks, the soles of their shoes, the cuffs of their jerseys and jackets, their pencils and books, were all sticky.

◇

On her second day (she had spent the first one in a sort of numb daze), Fraulein Angelika had started a shopping list. *Soap* it said, at the top.

◇

And now it was day three, the bucket was in place, there was an ominous fizzing at the back of Fraulein Angelika's nose that felt like the beginning of a sneeze, and on her desk was a pile of papers. They were greyish pages of very hard-to-read writing, some of it cramped, some sprawling, some wandering across the page like water running down a hill. All sticky. The one that Fraulein Angelika was reading at that moment was of the cramped kind, and the writer had pressed very hard, so that the pencil had made grooves in the paper.

Fraulein Angelika had not thought very hard about the essay title she had given to her class. In fact, she had picked the first that came into her head: 'What I Did in the Holidays'.

And so she read:

What I Did in the Holidays
and
Why Hansel's Jacket Is So Tight
(by Gretel, aged 10)

What I did in the holidays, Gretel had written,
was I shouted, 'Hurry, hurry, Hansel!' and
we ran all the way back home with the heaps
of treasure . . .

Fraulein Angelika paused to look at Gretel. Already in her mind she had divided the schoolroom into sections. The back-row desks: half asleep, the oldest children, and the most in need of soap. The middle-row desks: awake, but terrible suckers of pencils and fingers. The front row: the least sticky and best dressed, especially the girl with the pink frock and ridiculous name who could not say the letter 'R' and had such a breathless way of speaking. 'I like 'withmatic,' she had panted to Fraulein Angelika, 'better than witing! Have you wead my witing yet?' She had round sky-blue eyes and yellow curls, which she flounced.

Gretel, who sat at one of the middle-row desks, had no curls to flounce. Gretel had thin greenish-brown braids with ragged ends, and a greenish-brown dress with ragged pockets. She was sucking her pencil, the pointed end, which left a damp ring of grey round her mouth.

She did not look like she had recently run anywhere with heaps of treasure, and yet she had written:

Pearls and gold money. That was what was in the boxes we found at the witch's house. We stuffed our pockets full of treasure and I carried a lot more held up in my skirt and Hansel filled his hat like a bag and we ran and ran and ran and Hurray! we found the way home!

Father was so pleased to see us and we spilt the treasure all over the floor and the pearls bounced and the gold rolled and it looked very pretty.

'Now can Hansel and me live happily ever after with you?' I said to Father and he said, 'Yes you can! And your stepmother is dead and you know how much I love you. Where did you get the treasure from?'

'We stole it from the witch,' I said. 'She is dead as well, so it doesn't matter we did.'

Fraulein Angelika primly inserted 'that' before 'we did', added lots of commas, and drew red circles around the worst of the mistakes. The drip bucket slowly filled. The pink-dressed girl sucked the blue bead necklace she wore around her neck. Someone gave a mighty sniff.

Half the class had colds, and hardly any of them seemed to own handkerchiefs.

Something for Their Noses, Fraulein Angelika wrote on the shopping list, underneath *Soap*. (Was she going to sneeze, or wasn't she? Not, thought Fraulein Angelika firmly.)

The witch was horrible to Hansel and me, Gretel had written. *Her oven went BANG! after I pushed her in. I had to push her in because do you know what she said to me? 'Stick your head in the oven, Gretel, and see if it is hot enough!' Which was all cheating and pretending because she knew it was hot. All morning she had made me put sticks in the fire underneath it until it shone bright red when you opened the door. But I was cleverer than the witch because I said, 'We don't have an oven at home. We just have a kettle and make toast. I don't know how to tell how hot is hot enough.' Then the witch was taken in by my cleverness and she said, 'You see if an oven is hot enough by sticking your head in LIKE THIS!'*

So she did and quick as a flash I shoved hard on her knobbly old bottom and in she went and I slammed the door shut and I ran

outside fast and a good job too because it
went BANG! like I said and the chimney shot
up into the sky like a rocket when you have
fireworks and black smoke came out and
red and green sparks and that was the witch
burning up.

'Gretel, dear,' said Fraulein Angelika.

'What, miss?' said Gretel.

'You seem to have written this story backwards.'

'It's not a story, miss,' said Gretel.

'You have begun with the last thing that happened,' persisted Fraulein Angelika. 'It's a very good story, but it would be even better if you had started with the first thing that happened. And Gretel, I'm sure it isn't good for you to suck your pencil so much.'

'It makes it blacker,' said Gretel. 'It isn't black enough, else.'

'It isn't black enough, *otherwise*,' corrected Fraulein Angelika.

'I know,' agreed Gretel.

So good news, the witch was dead and we
didn't cook Hansel after all and I ran and let
him out of his cage in the stable. Hansel had
been in the cage for three weeks . . .

No oven at home, thought Fraulein Angelika Maria, looking across the room at Gretel. Only toast and a kettle. No wonder the child was so thin. Hansel, on the other hand, her nine-year-old brother, was quite different. So tightly packed into his shabby brown jacket that the buttons pulled in the buttonholes like dogs on a lead. It was a mystery. Or was it?

Fraulein Angelika read on:

The witch was trying to make Hansel fat and when he was fat enough she was going to cook him and eat him and that's why the oven had to be so hot. I wasn't going to eat him, but I had to help cook. I don't know why the witch wanted to eat Hansel. She had plenty of other food. She had more food than anyone else I ever knew and she cooked and cooked all the time. She gave most of her cooking to Hansel. That's why his jacket is so tight, miss. But luckily the witch couldn't see that Hansel's jacket was tight. She had very bad eyes and she could hardly make out Hansel in his little cage. So she used to say, 'Stick out your finger, Hansel, so I can see if it's time to cook you yet.'

But Hansel did not stick out his finger. Instead he stuck out a bone, a chicken bone,

*from some chicken soup that the witch had
made. I found it when I was washing the
soup pot and I gave it to Hansel and told him
what to do. He would never have thought
of it himself, not in that cage. He was too
frightened to think in the witch's house,
although usually he is clever. But he was not
clever there. He just ate. He ate porridge with
cream and eggs with ham and cheese and
butter and puddings and cake.*

No fruit, thought Fraulein Angelika Maria. No
vegetables. No salad. Salad made her think of her
favourite restaurant in the city, where they served

delicious salads on curved white plates, and pale gold wine in tall fragile glasses. She and her friends had met there for a farewell lunch, only a few days before. Her friends had all clinked glasses and laughed and called, 'Good luck, Angelika Maria! You are mad! He's definitely not worth it! But good luck!'

'It will be a wonderful adventure! I adore the countryside! The air! The flowers! Orchids!' she had said, caressing the stem of pale green orchids in the vase on the table. 'You know I love orchids, and they are so expensive to buy here in the city. Imagine picking them wild!'

'Surely not in autumn?' someone had wondered. 'Surely it's mostly mud in autumn?'

But then lots of other people had chimed in to say that they had often bought orchids in autumn, and roses and lilies and violets too, and they must come from somewhere.

'Of course they must,' agreed Angelika Maria. 'And the children *will* be adorable. Bliss!'

It seemed so far from the forest, and so long ago, as to be the memory of a dream.

The witch was a very good cook, for a witch,
continued Gretel's extremely black writing,
and when me and Hansel first found her
house she seemed a kind old lady. 'Come

in, little children, come in out of the cold,'
she said, when she found us eating her
windowsill. She wasn't cross at all, although
we ate quite a lot of it, and we ate a corner of
the roof too and Hansel licked the windows.
He said they were made of barley sugar but I
didn't try them.

At this point the blanket of dullness over Fraulein Angelika Maria lifted once again. Barley-sugar windows! What a wonderful imagination! Gretel must be encouraged with her writing, thought Fraulein Angelika. She must be shown how to tell a story from the beginning, as well as from the end, and she must not be made ill from the consumption of pencils. *Edible Pencils*, Fraulein Angelika wrote on her shopping list, and she was about to search through the pages on her desk for Hansel's *What I Did in the Holidays*, to see if he was equally talented, when she was distracted by a paper with no proper work on it at all.

Just the name *Jack* at the top, and a single sentence:

'Mam says us will have to sell our Sukey.'

The paper was distinctly damp, as well as sticky. Fraulein Angelika Maria rightly deduced that the blots were tears.

'Which one is Jack?' she asked, for except for the jacket-bursting Hansel, the boys all looked very much alike to her.

A stringy-looking person with very close-together eyes blinked and said, 'Me, miss. What, miss?'

'How are you getting on, Jack?' said Fraulein Angelika, thinking how much he looked like a burglar. 'Are you managing your work?'

'No, miss,' said Jack. 'Not really.'

'Then you must let me help,' said Fraulein Angelika. 'That's what I am here for.'

Jack's mouth dropped open in surprise, but his eyes looked suddenly much brighter, and after a moment of gathering his thoughts he said all the fences could do with a patch, and there was a haystack needed shifting, and if they could get the back field dug over then they might put in some winter beet.

At this point Gretel gave him a sharp shove with a very bony elbow and hissed, 'She can't do nothing like that!'

'She said that's what she were here for,' hissed Jack, shoving back.

'She's not got the clothes for it!'

'Us could find her some overalls,' said Jack stubbornly. 'You mind your own, Gretel! Us could find you some overalls, miss, and a fork for the hay.'

'I meant help with your arithmetic, Jack,' said

Fraulein Angelika, as patiently as she could manage, 'if you are finding it difficult.'

'I done the sums,' said Jack ungratefully. 'I done them easy. Sums is a sitting-down job. I wouldn't mind doing sums all day. Did you see what I wrote you about our Sukey, miss?'

'Yes I did,' said Fraulein Angelika, and took from her bag a second snow-white linen handkerchief, handed it to him for his tears, and tactfully turned her attention to Hansel while he mopped.

Hansel's jacket was so tight that he could hardly bend his arms.

'Hansel, would you be more comfortable if you took that jacket off?' asked Fraulein Angelika.

'I've not got nothing underneath, miss,' said Hansel, sounding shocked.

'I haven't got *anything* underneath,' corrected Fraulein Angelika Maria, and Hansel looked even more shocked and blushed bright red and would not look at her.

'I got a vest!' murmured Gretel, proudly.

'I got a vest and a petticoat!' said the fat little girl with the curls.

Fraulein Angelika Maria resisted the very strong temptation to join in with, 'I've got a French silk camisole, peach with satin embroidery,' and said, 'Quiet please, girls!' instead.

Hansel's 'What I Did in the Holidays' began:

Our stepmother said there wasn't no more food hardly. Only enough for her and our father and none for Gretel and me. Be best, she said, if our father was to take us off and get us lost in the forest so we never came back no more. O my poor children said our father. It is for the best, said our stepmother. Trust me because I am always right.

Our stepmother never knew we heard because she sent us to bed but we listened through the holes in the floor. Gretel cried. Do not cry Gretel, I said. Do not worry because I will make a plan.

For my plan I got up very early and I collected in my pocket a lot of little white stones, all the little white stones I could find around our house. I was very happy when I had my pockets full of stones and I whispered to Gretel, 'It is going to be all right, Gretel,' and Gretel believed me and she stopped crying.

So that morning our father and our stepmother took Gretel and me deep and far into the forest, and when we got a long way from home they lit a fire and said, 'Stay here till we come back.' And they didn't come back and night came and there were stars over the *trees and the moon was shining.*

But with the little white stones I had made a trail, right from our house and in the moonlight they shone bright and we could see them and we followed them all the way home.

Now what shall we do? said Gretel.

We will knock on the door, I said, and we knocked on the door.

The End

'Hansel,' said Fraulein Angelika Maria, 'I have your essay here on my desk, but it does not seem to be finished. You have written *The End*, but it cannot be the end.'

Hansel peered at her from under his thatch of shaggy brown hair. His eyes were round and dark. They did not show his thoughts.

'It was going so well, with the stones and the moonlight,' continued Fraulein Angelika Maria. 'It was getting quite exciting. Wouldn't you like to write some more?'

'No, miss,' said Hansel, shaking his head. And just as he spoke the clock on the wall behind Fraulein Angelika Maria began to strike twelve and the whole class, that had a second before looked sleepily, firmly, fixed to their seats forever, erupted into boots and clatter and hoods and reaching arms and falling books and the door pulled open and let in a gale of wet air.

Bong! went the last strike of twelve o'clock, and every child in the room had vanished.

On the first day that this happened, Fraulein Angelika Maria had been so frozen with shock she had not moved for the entire lunch hour. On the second day, she had run after the class, shrieking. Now, on this, the third, day, she simply opened her bag and took out her lunchtime apple. It was a very red and lovely one, wrapped up in crisp tissue paper, one of a box that her friends had given her as a goodbye present. Fraulein Angelika thought of those friends in the city (who were probably only just out of bed). She thought of her dreadful ex-boyfriend, who had said, in cold blood, on her birthday, that he thought he'd never get a better bargain than his wonderful mother, with whom he intended to live forever. She thought, with satisfaction, that at least she'd pushed him into the river, since they were handily standing on a bridge. She remembered how cross she'd been at the time when a heroic policeman dived in and fished him out.

Although, admitted Fraulein Angelika Maria to herself, it would have been very inconvenient if he'd drowned. Prison! Me? And now here I am, a million miles from civilization, to prove that I do not care if the ridiculous man lives with his mother till he's ninety!

And I don't care either, thought Fraulein Angelika Maria. And I can even see that some of the children might really be adorable. Hansel, anyway. But they are so incredibly sticky and they will come back after lunch even stickier. If only there was a spare drip bucket, they could wash their hands in the full one . . . I could warm it on the stove . . .

Spare Drip Bucket, wrote Fraulein Angelika Maria triumphantly on her shopping list. Then, finishing her apple, she turned back to Gretel's story:

> *The windowsills of the witch's house were made of gingerbread. I ate a lot of windowsill while Hansel was licking the barley-sugar windows. It tasted a bit mouldy but I was so hungry I didn't care. The roof was nicer. It had sugar-icing patterns. There was so much wood in the forest it seemed silly to build a house of gingerbread, but that was what the witch did. The other thing wrong with having a house made out of gingerbread is what about when it rains? It would go soggy. And why didn't rats and mice and birds eat it up? And foxes and bears? Perhaps it was a trap for children like Hansel and me. But I don't suppose many children go that far into the forest.*
>
> *Hansel and I only went so far because we were lost. We couldn't find Hansel's*

breadcrumbs. *Do not think Hansel was not brave, miss , because he was so frightened at the witch's house. Anyone would be frightened if they were locked up in a cage and fattened up for a witch's dinner. Until that happened Hansel was the bravest of the brave.*

I'm sure he was, agreed Fraulein Angelika, nodding.

At that moment, the schoolroom clock struck one. The door burst open. All the children rushed back in and flumped down at their desks, stickier than ever, as

Fraulein Angelika Maria had known they would. But now she was no longer under her terrible cloud. Now she had a plan. *Towels*, she wrote on her shopping list, *Pink and Blue (with spares). Floor Polish, Desk Polish, Dusters. Window Boxes, Lettuce Seeds. Compasses (one each, so they don't get lost in the forest)* . . .

Goodness! thought Fraulein Angelika Maria. There is so much to do, and I have only got a year, and nearly three days gone already! Gretel is clearly a genius, and Hansel is actually a cherub!! (*New Jacket for Hansel*, she wrote on her shopping list). That little girl in pink must be taught to say her 'Rs'. None of them seem to know how to sing . . . (*Song Books*, she wrote on the shopping list), or how to play (*Skipping Ropes, Balls, Storybooks*). A piano would be useful . . .

Piano, Fraulein Angelika wrote. She adored shopping. She could hardly wait to begin, but meanwhile there was afternoon school, and an empty seat beside Gretel.

'Where is Jack?' asked Fraulein Angelika Maria.

'He's not coming back this afternoon, miss,' said Gretel, 'because of taking their Sukey to market.'

'He can't just miss school like that!' exclaimed Fraulein Angelika Maria. 'I should have had a note.'

'He said he gave you one,' said Gretel.

Fraulein Angelika looked down at the dampest and stickiest piece of paper on her desk, and realized that he had.

'He's not had to go all the way to market, though,' continued Gretel. 'He met a man who wanted to buy her almost as soon as he started. So he sold her for five beans.'

'Gretel,' said Fraulein Angelika Maria, in a very pleased voice, 'you are telling a story forwards! That's very good indeed! If Jack sold Sukey so quickly he should have come back to school.'

'It's not a story,' said Gretel, 'and he didn't come back, because he thought he'd better give the beans to his mother in case they got lost.'

'Very sensible,' said Fraulein Angelika Maria. 'Did his mother want beans so much?'

'She didn't want them at all,' said Gretel. 'She said they wasn't magic and she throwed them out the window.'

'She *threw* them out of the window.'

'I didn't know you knew,' said Gretel. 'Did you hear her shouting? She'll be surprised in the morning when they grow into a beanstalk with a castle on the top.'

'Miss, have you wead my witing yet?' asked the little girl in pink.

'I have,' said Fraulein Angelika, 'and we must talk about how to spell "porridge". It is a word full of "Rs" not "Ws". But first I have to bring the register up to date. I know about Jack.

'Does anyone know why Punzel, R has not been in school this term?'

'She's been stuck up a tower for ages,' said Gretel.

'Oh Gretel, really! And Simon and Dick?'

'Simon went off with a goose, and Dick went off with a cat,' said Hansel.

'Beauty, the merchant's daughter?'

'She's living with a beast. Her father took her,' chorused half the class.

'Absent, absent, absent, and absent,' Fraulein Angelika noted in the register, 'and none of them with a proper excuse.' Living with a beast, her father took her indeed! thought Fraulein Angelika indignantly. I absolutely *must* organize a parents' evening!

'Is it sums again this afternoon, miss?' asked Hansel.

'No Hansel, it is Art,' said Fraulein Angelika, 'and Art is something so long to be learned, as the philosophers tell us, that we will begin at once. Gretel, please hand out crayons and paper. I should like you each to draw me a picture of My Family and My Favourite Pet.'

'What if you just live with dwarves?' asked a dark-haired girl from one of the middle-row seats.

'Then draw the dwarves,' said Fraulein Angelika.

'All of them?' asked the girl.

'You may have two sheets of drawing paper,' said Fraulein Angelika kindly. 'Now then, Goldilocks, *porridge*! I've written it here in big letters, so come and show me the "Rs"!'

The second time they took us into the forest
Hansel did not have time to find stones. He
broke up his piece of bread instead, and
scattered a trail of breadcrumbs

We went much further the second time;
we walked for hours and hours and hours
until it was like walking and being asleep
at the same time. I do remember a pile of
brown leaves and they looked so comfortable
I thought I would lie down for just a minute
and then I would hurry and catch them up
but I went asleep for too long. When I woke
up it was black dark and Hansel was asleep
beside me and our father and our stepmother
had gone.

The breadcrumbs had gone too. The birds
had eaten them up.

The first time we were lost in the forest we
got home again the next day by following
Hansel's white stones and we arrived at the
house at morning and then I didn't know
what to do but Hansel knocked on the door
and it was our father and he hugged us tight.
But I saw our stepmother behind him. I saw
her face. She was not glad that we had found
our way back. She said we ate too much
food. We heard her talking one night through

*the holes in the floor. She said there wasn't
enough food and so Hansel and me must be
taken into the forest and lost. That was how
it all began and that is why Hansel's jacket is
so tight.*

The End.

Fraulein Angelika Maria could not help it. It was too
sad. Her eyes filled with tears and her nose prickled
dreadfully and she realized that she was going to sneeze
at last. She felt blindly for her bag and discovered that
she had no more handkerchiefs. 'Oh dear,' she said
unhappily, and sniffed.

Gretel was watching her. Gretel reached into her
ragged pocket and pulled out a ragged bundle, a
collection of little bits and pieces all wrapped in a
handkerchief.

'Here, miss!' she said, tipping out the collection, and
she pushed the handkerchief into Fraulein Angelika's
hand.

She was just in time. Fraulein Angelika took a huge
breath, closed her streaming eyes, and sneezed an
enormous sneeze.

'Thank you, Gretel,' she said gratefully, when she had
recovered. 'Thank you! Whatever should I have done if
you had not been there! And Gretel, you have written a
wonderful story!'

She dabbed her eyes with the handkerchief and blinked.

Gazed . . . and blinked again.

A handful of pearls, a dozen or more gold coins, sticky but shining, on her desk.

She looked at them for a long, long time, and then she looked at Gretel.

'It wasn't a story, Gretel,' said Fraulein Angelika.

'No, miss,' said Gretel.

10

Sweet William by Rushlight
or
The Swan Brothers

A rushlight was a poor person's light on a dark night. It was made from the pith at the centre of the stiff green rushes that grew, and still grow, near marshy ground. The green outside was peeled away to leave the white pith, which was dipped in wax or tallow and then allowed to dry. A good rushlight might burn for half an hour or more.

They are easy to make. I have made them now and then myself for fun. You need to leave a green strip on the pith to stiffen it, and if you allow it to dry for a few hours before dipping it in your wax, then you get a longer-lasting light. But you can never tell with a rushlight. Some burn long, and some burn short.

◊

I have seven rushlights to tell my story by.

◊

This story has been told so many times. So many voices, so many memories, that the facts have been lost in the telling. How many brothers were there? Was it nettles or starflowers that were woven, and what was the name of the girl? Was it swans, or crows? And how many days, or was it years?

Well, I was there, and this is my chance to write down the truth. With a swan-feather quill and seven rushlights to lighten the darkness.

There were seven brothers.

Nettles were woven.

Her name was Elsa.

Swans.

It took seven years.

◊

There were seven brothers, and they were princes of a small kingdom, mostly forest, mostly happy. The princes were born in pairs: Jacob and Joseph; Lucas and Mark; Timon and Toby, and then me. I was the youngest. I was Will.

Will, Sweet William, Billy-O.

Jacob and Joseph, they were our leaders, born, said our mother, at the moment the sun sprang into the sky. Jacob and Joseph were seldom to be found within the castle walls. Always, from little boys, they were away along the forest rides or out amongst the villages. Tireless and merry and everyone's friends. If there was a field to be reaped, a fire to be tamed, a child wandered away needing

Jacob and Joseph

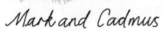

William and Elsa

Mark and Cadmus

Timon and Toby

Lucas

to be found, a flood to be forged, a horse to be ridden, then Jacob and Joseph were there. The villagers loved them, but not more than we did. When they returned to the castle, you'd know it was because there was nothing left to do. They'd stagger sometimes as they led their horses across the courtyard, and they'd be soaked from a river or red-eyed from fire and they'd fall asleep in their supper bowls. They were good boys.

Lucas was our minstrel, thin and dark-eyed. He carried his lute across his back so as never to have to hunt for it, and he kept a flute in his pocket. He had a talent for making little clay birds, hollow inside with a reed for a tail. With a drop of water inside and a breath down the reed, they would bubble and sing like a hedge full of finches. Half the children for miles had a little clay bird, and the rest had cuckoo-callers, cut from hollow stems. Lucas was a great whistler himself; he had ever a melody, you always knew he was near.

Different to Mark! You'd think you were alone till you heard a laugh at your shoulder and there would be Mark. And at Mark's side would be his great golden hound, Cadmus. The day Mark learned to walk they took him outside to practise on the soft grass, where it didn't hurt to fall. *Stagger, stagger, wobble, wobble,* went Mark across the lawn, and tumbled through a gap in the beech hedge. Up jumped our mother, and up jumped Jacob and Joseph, but before they could take a step he was back. On his feet again, and walking much steadier this time, leaning as he was on the shoulder of a hound so huge that at first sight they took him to be a lion. But Cadmus was no lion. He was a dog. One of the ageless companions of the fortunate that step out of legends now and then to remind us that our deeds don't go unwatched. Cadmus and Mark! Mark grew from a child to a man, but Cadmus might have been a painted picture, for all he seemed to change.

The last set of twins was Timon and Toby. Toby, our court jester, dark eyes and apple cheeks and forever erupting into laughter. Timon was our dreamer, with his head full of stories. Those two were always together. Give Toby a cake, and he'd hand it straight to Timon. And if Timon caught a cold, it was Toby who would sneeze.

I was the last of the brothers, a plain boy in a brown jacket, with scuffed boots and a knitted cap. But it wasn't a plain life with brothers like mine, and I never missed not having a twin, because after me came Elsa.

Elsa, our little sister.

Our father used to ask a riddle: if I have seven boys and a sister for each of them, how many children have I?

Elsa was a sister for each of us.

Jacob and Joseph taught her to ride, and up she would go on the saddle behind them, to ride out to the villages in the morning. She would sing with Lucas, clear and sweet like a winter robin, and she would listen to Timon's stories with her lips parted in astonishment and wide grey eyes. Toby made her laugh until she had to rush out of the room, and Mark would dance with her, but who taught her to curtsy afterwards? A careful dip to Mark and then a slow deep sweep to Cadmus.

But with me she was my best friend ever, my keeper of secrets, my comrade in arms. I lent her my jacket when she was cold and she shared her apples and biscuits with me, and together we read many books, and fell out of many trees, and tracked many creatures across the snow, and pondered over many pictures, on our stomachs before the fire in wintertime, flat on our backs in the meadow in summer, squinting through our fingers to count the butterflies.

Then our mother died.

◇

Six rushlights left.

◇

Our mother died in the deep of winter, on a day when great grey flakes fell from the faded sky and all colour was buried on the earth.

We clung to each other that day, and after we shivered for a while.

But not forever. Jacob and Joseph straightened their shoulders and looked out into the world to find the next place that they were needed. Timon remembered his stories. 'Dark and light,' said Timon. 'That's how they go. No light without dark, now and then.' He looked up at Toby, and Toby, who was born to smile, smiled down at him.

And Lucas discovered that the children in the villages still needed their clay birds, and that his lute still needed its tunes. Also Mark was still brave enough for a hero's hound, and Elsa was still a sister to each of us. I remember she took my cold hands in her two warm ones and said, 'Don't be sad, Will, Sweet William, Billy-O. I will take care of you now.'

So spring came and the snow went and we came alive again.

But our father did not.

Our father stayed in his winter despair, his mind a tangle of sadness and worry, and he paced the floors and the castle grounds and the roads and the paths through the forest and he wrung his hands and said, 'What can I do? What can I do? Joseph and Jacob so reckless. Lucas so pale. Mark lost without that beast, and Timon with his head in the clouds. Toby never sensible for two moments together. And Will . . . more like a boy from the cottages than a prince. And Elsa! A girl needs a mother.'

'Elsa, look at you!' he would say, and then Elsa would hurry to wash her hands and untangle her brown curls and she would try and walk primly amongst us for a while.

It was not enough for my father though.

There is no easy way to put this, so I will have to choose the plain way.

He married a witch.

A witch, but not a hag. As fair a witch as you would find within the ringing of a bell. A heart-melting smile, and a way with her eyes when she tilted her head. Swift-stepped and golden-haired, and suddenly the swish and sigh of silken skirts in the castle again.

◊

Well!

Some polishing was done that summer! Some corners were swept! It was not long before our castle was a very different place. Lilies in the flowerbeds where our mother had grown her roses.

A very powerful witch. Between sunrise and sunset Cadmus vanished, and Mark went very quiet.

Then there was the baby. Yellow-headed as a dandelion amongst all of us brown boys. Our little brother, I suppose, although we rarely saw him. He was kept away from us. Even Elsa, who would have loved him, was hardly allowed by him. I didn't like the way the witch spoke to Elsa.

'Are you clean?' she would say.

Elsa would hold out her washed pink hands.

'Curtsy then, to greet him.'

Elsa would bob a friendly curtsy and hold out her hands.

'Come Dandelion! Come Dandy! Come to Elsa!'

'His name is Florian.'

'Come Florian, into the garden.'

'He may not go into the garden.'

'Where may he play with me?'

'He does not need to play. Curtsy and take your leave.'

◇

'Poor Florian!' Elsa said to us afterwards. 'He's just a little boy. But when I said that to his mother, she said, "He is not a little boy; he is a future king." What did she mean?' asked Elsa, and she looked at us, her seven brothers, seven future kings before Florian, and her eyes were very anxious.

'They were just words,' said Jacob.

'Empty,' said Joseph.

'Nothing,' said Lucas . . . although Mark remained silent.

'Silly,' said Toby, looking at Timon.

And Timon agreed. 'A dream.'

'He's just a little boy,' I said. 'A dandelion head.'

We forgot she was a witch.

◇

Five rushlights left.

◇

273

Our father said to us, 'I am sending you boys to the old hunting lodge in the forest.'

'No you're not,' said Joseph.

'I am sending you boys to the old hunting lodge in the forest,' repeated our father, bewitched if ever a man was.

'For why?' asked Jacob.

'Elsa is there already,' said our father. 'Alone.'

'Alone?' roared Mark. 'What do you mean, alone?'

'I am sending you boys to the old hunting lodge in the forest,' said our father, in the same empty voice. 'Elsa is there already. Alone.'

Jacob and Joseph were already gone, saddled in record time, and galloping. Mark and Lucas were not far behind, and Toby and Timon were racing for the stables.

I ran too. I had a dappled pony in those days; Pebble he was called. He lived in the meadow and he didn't like being caught. He didn't like it that day better than any other, so I was the last away from the castle.

Around our castle there ran a swift river, and across the river was a wide stone bridge. Over the bridge, and the world was before you: towns and villages and forest and meadow. It was the gateway in and the gateway out, and on it the witch stood watching, and her child was with her, watching too.

Pebble was running, although not quick enough for

me. I was standing in the stirrups, urging him to be faster, when I heard a dreadful shriek.

And although I was, like my brothers, on fire with anger that morning, that shriek ran cold as ice through my veins.

Then it came again, and a moan of despair.

The witch's child, dandelion-headed Florian, had slipped and fallen. A witch's power does not hold over running water, and she was helpless as she watched. He was in the river, tumbling and rolling, sinking and bobbing up, flailing and then swept down again by the rushing water. Two years old and drowning.

But I was a sturdy twelve, and I was in that river after him before I had time to think. By great good luck I caught him by his dandelion hair. The water was deep and very cold, and we were buffeted more than once against the brown rocks that churned the current. But I held on tight and shielded him as best I could. Far down the river I fought my way to the bank at last with the witch's child in my arms.

I turned him upside down then, and half the river poured from him, but he was alive.

The witch arrived, and she grabbed him from me like she thought I might throw him back. Then she stared into my face and her eyes were blazing with witchcraft and hate and another look too that I could not name.

'What do you want?' she asked.

'Get him warm,' I told her, my teeth rattling with the cold, and she turned away.

I wrung the water out of my jacket as best I could, and managed to catch and mount Pebble at last, and I followed the road my brothers had taken, away into the forest to the old hunting lodge that stood on the border of our little kingdom. A damp and musty tumbledown place it was.

Still is.

◇

One night we had with Elsa.

And then the full moon and then the spell.

Witches are witches all the earth over. Their greatest power comes with the brightest moon.

It must have taken great power to weave that spell.

She wove us into swans.

◇

Four rushlights left.

◇

To be a boy, and then a swan!

To fall asleep within shadowy walls, and to wake in the morning sky, beating east into the sunrise, and far beneath you white wisps of lambswool that are clouds, and as you gaze at them you become aware of such vast height, and a drop so blue, so blue and distant as to turn your heart.

Far beneath us was the tumbling ocean.

And the ice whistle of the wind, and the *creak, creak* of huge white wings, and in front of me and beside me my brothers, snow-white swans.

That perilous first morning of flight, it brought such joy as I had never felt before. It came from the lift of the air; the great steady rhythm of lift and beat, and lift and beat.

Never in my warm, sweet, earthbound life as a boy had I known such bliss.

But we were flying for our lives; there was no land in sight and no rest for us on that wild ocean. We were weary to our hollow swan bones when we saw the island.

It was hardly an island in truth, no more than a large rock and enormous waves breaking all around. But we rested there for the night and journeyed on the next morning and we came at last to a far country, east of the sunrise.

There were no people in that land. It was a world of spreading pools and rushes and dragonflies and enormous skies. We drifted on those clear pools with our swan reflections always beside us, and our thoughts were swan thoughts, of water and wind and sky. But each night the moon diminished from the full, until one night it was as slim as a curved blade, and the next it was gone.

Witches are witches all the skies over. Their power fades as the moon fades. In the night with no moon we became human again, and we found our voices. We looked at each other and said, 'Elsa.'

But the morning found us swans again, with swan thoughts loud in our minds. One thing, though: we had learned to watch the moon.

It grew in the night skies, from a thin blade to a bright full moon, and then we were wholly swans and we spread far from each other amongst the pools and into the heights. At those times I could not have told you my name.

But a full moon wanes, and as it did we remembered. It faded back to a half and then a quarter, and we gathered, knowing something was changing. When it was once more approaching the blade, we remembered our home. And when it was just two days from the night without moon, we knew the way back and we summoned our courage to our long swan wings and set off across the ocean.

Together we made the journey. A day to the rock, and a day to the home shore, and by nightfall at this old hunting lodge, and voices again and human form. The weight of the earth a great drag on the body after all those weeks as a swan.

Six weeks Elsa had waited.

Have you forgotten Cadmus?

I had.

But Elsa had Cadmus, and when we had done hugging her, we turned to hugging him.

'I knew you would come back,' said Elsa.

It was my turn to hold her and I buried my face in her hair.

'Don't worry!' she said. 'Don't be sad, Sweet William! I know what to do. Cadmus was watching when she wove the spell.'

We looked at Cadmus then, and before our eyes he became a little fox, a golden bee, a spark of light.

Then back through the changes and a hound again.

'Cadmus says all spells have a counter-spell to balance them. And the counter-spell to Seven Swan

Princes is Seven Nettle Shirts. And I am to weave them, and I must work the weaving in silence, and when they are finished they will set you free. I can weave,' said Elsa proudly, 'and spin and sew. But I can't stay here. There are no nettles in the forest, I've looked.'

She was nine years old.

'Elsa,' said Joseph gently, 'you can't weave nettles.'

'The country people do,' said Elsa.

'Nettles sting,' said Jacob.

'So does sadness,' said Elsa.

'We can't have you hurt,' said Lucas.

'I can't have you swans.'

'No, Elsa,' said Mark and Toby and Timon.

'No, Elsa,' said I, with my face in her hair.

But Elsa laid her finger on her lips and did not reply.

◊

Three rushlights left.

◊

We woke the next morning as we had woken the first time as swans. High in the sky, flying east.

It was many years before we saw Elsa again.

We searched. Each month, in the last day of the waning moon, we gathered and flew west to reach the old land in time for a few hours in human form. We made those journeys many times, and they each had their own peril. I only have three rushlights left, so leave that unwritten.

Each month we would go amongst the people, asking and listening. Not our own people, you understand. We wanted no rumours reaching the castle and the witch, but still, we heard the news.

We learned many things.

Of the search by the country folk for Elsa and the lost princes.

Of the death of our father and the ruling of the Witch Queen.

Of the trouble she brought, the failed harvests and the emptying villages.

And at last, in a neighbouring kingdom, we heard of a silent girl who wove nettles.

'Had she a hound?' asked Mark eagerly, and they said, not a hound but a small gold fox.

Then gradually we learned more of the story.

◊

Elsa had been seen by huntsmen on the borders of a neighbouring kingdom. A brown-haired girl with a bundle of nettles in her arms. If I had more rushlights I would write more of this, how she slept in the treetops, only climbing down for more nettles, and how the fox brought her bread every morning.

'How did the fox find the bread?' I asked her once.

'How did the hound become a fox?' she replied. 'How did the fox become a bee? How did the bee become a shining spark in my hair? How did seven princes become seven swans? Do you know, Billy-O?'

'I don't,' I said.

Well, in the end the huntsmen caught her, and they took her where they took all their best catches, to the Queen who ruled the neighbouring kingdom. There Elsa stayed, in the Royal Court, and there she spun and wove her nettles. Not the whole nettle, you understand, but the long fibres in the nettle stems, after the leaves were plucked away. The fibres spun into a pale green thread, and the thread woven into a fair green cloth.

They told me later that all the long years she spun and wove, she never spoke a word or hummed a song or sighed a whisper, and there was a small golden bee in her hair.

At first she amused them at the palace, so small, so quick to smile, so careful in her spinning, so uncomplaining of her sore, stung hands. They found she could dance, and ride. Sometimes she put aside her weaving to make small hollow birds out of clay for visiting children. She would dip them full of water and laugh when the children learned to blow them to make birdsong – but she never made a sound herself.

She grew more beautiful each year, and the Queen's son fell in love with her and he said he would marry her. But Elsa measured the lengths of woven cloth in her store, and shook her head, and she watched the sky, morning and night.

Now, when Elsa first came to that country, there had grown as many nettles there as anywhere else. But not any longer. There were no nettles now in the parks and gardens and farms and lanes, they were all gathered and spun and woven. And Elsa measured the lengths of nettle cloth and shook her head. She needed more.

There was one place left and it was forbidden: an old graveyard with a high wall. A thousand years of kings and queens lay sleeping there, with their rings and staffs and golden crowns, and nettles grew through the glinting green mounds.

The penalty for trespass there was death.

But Elsa climbed the wall.

And so she was caught and imprisoned to await her fate, and the Queen's son begged, and the lawyers shook their heads, and by a golden spark of light behind the prison walls, Elsa sewed her nettle cloth into pale shirts.

Then her verdict came: death for robbing the dead, and the Queen's son could not bear it and he said he would die with her. And there came a morning when they led her out to her fate.

Even then Elsa would not be parted from her work. She carried in her arms the nettle shirts, greeny-gold they shone in the sunlight, and no one could get near her because with her was a great golden hound.

◇

Two rushlights left.

It was a hound in form, but not in size. It was as huge and swift as twenty hounds, and around its feet screeched and snapped a hundred golden foxes and in the air swarmed furious bees and the whole court crackled and spat with fiery sparks and it was the day before the dark of the moon.

Mark was leading. Seven years a swan now, and with such power in his wings as could thrust the clouds apart, and Cadmus in the courtyard below. The spitting golden light and the terrible deep thunder of his baying.

Mark shot through blue distances like a great white arrow, and we followed after, and there was Elsa at last.

She ran to us as we flew to her.

Jacob and Joseph, Mark and Lucas, Timon and Toby. Over each of them as they came winging towards her she flung a green nettle shirt, and their swan shapes left them and they stood on the earth as men. Then it was my turn and the last shirt for me.

Afterwards Elsa said it was because she had so little cloth the last sleeve was short. Maybe, maybe not. I know that I flinched away as it touched me, and it slid from my left shoulder.

Swan Wing, they call me. I have been William Swan Wing for many years now.

Elsa married the Queen's son and now she has her own princes and princesses.

    Jacob and Joseph ride less and move more slowly on their feet.

Mark and Lucas sit together in the sun.

Toby has grown round and Timon has grown thin, but Lucas still plays his lute now and then and Cadmus is as he ever was. Perhaps a little greyer around his muzzle.

It seems to me that the lightness has gone out of the days.

◇

One rushlight left.

◇

I remember the great lift of air under my wings. I remember the blue pools and the rushes. I remember the endless height and depth of the sky.

I remember the bliss of it all.

I heard a rumour. The witch was fading fast, they said.

And so I travelled back to the old country.

Now I've seen her.

She lies in bed as small as a child, shrunken with the years. Her voice is almost gone, and her eyes are closed.

'I'm Will,' I said. 'Remember me. I was the plain one.'

'You were,' she whispered.

'I've come to forgive you,' I said.

She turned her head, not wanting my forgiveness.

'Your boy?' I asked. 'Young Dandelion?'

Two tears slipped from the closed eyes.

'Gone?' I asked, speaking soft as I could. But she did not reply.

Better angry than sad, I thought then, so I changed the subject to rouse her up.

'This place has got right mucky,' I said. 'The windows all grime and the ceiling all webs and the lilies half choked in weeds.'

That worked. I saw her brace her shoulders with temper.

'I want to fly again,' I said. 'You owe me that. For my lost home and the seven years and my little sister alone and the long journeys, not knowing what had become of her.'

She said nothing.

'And for young Dandelion pulled out of the river.'

Long pause.

But I knew she remembered.

'Yes,' said the witch.

'You owe me.'

'I do owe you for that,' she said.

'Well then.'

'I have no longer the power,' she said. 'Not for wings.'

'Ah!' said I. 'But I only need one!'

Then she opened her eyes at last.

There was still fire blazing there, but this time there was no hate. Just the look that I had seen long before, when I handed her Dandy, all dripping with river.

'What's the moon?' she whispered.

'Near full,' I said.

'It will have to be full.'

'Tomorrow.'

'It won't hold for long.'

'So long as it gets me there,' I said.

'Ah,' she murmured, but her voice was full of doubt, and I could tell that she knew that great ocean with its small rocky island, and the reeds and rushes and blue pools of the country east of the sunrise. She knew them as well as I.

'Beyond reach.'

I don't know if it was her said that, or me.

Then we were quiet, though she was still looking at me.

'One wing,' she said at last.

'The sky,' I told her, taking hope again. 'That's where

I'm aiming! The wind in the heights and the blueness.'

'The blueness,' she murmured, remembering with me.

'Never mind what comes after.'

'Swan Wing,' she said, and smiled.

And so here I am, back at the old hunting lodge. Just for this night, for old time's sake and the memories.

Full moon tomorrow.

It was love in her eyes that I saw when she looked at me; I knew that before I left.

She said, 'You'll reach the sky, Swan Wing, Billy-O, Sweet William.'

◇

And that's my last rushlight gone.

About the Author

Hilary McKay is a critically acclaimed author who has won many awards, including the Guardian Children's Fiction Prize for her first novel, *The Exiles*, and the Whitbread (now the Costa) Award for *Saffy's Angel*. Hilary studied Botany and Zoology at the University of St Andrews, and worked as a biochemist before the draw of the pen became too strong and she decided to become a full-time writer. Hilary lives in Derbyshire with her family.

About the Illustrator

Sarah Gibb studied at Saint Martin's School of Art (now Central Saint Martins) before completing her MA in Illustration at Brighton College of Art. After landing regular spots in the *Telegraph* and *Elle* magazine, Sarah went on to illustrate Sue Townsend's Adrian Mole series, many classic children's fairy tales and even the Harrods Christmas window display. She lives in Wandsworth, London.

Bibliography/Further Reading

These are some of the books that helped me write this collection:

Bernhardt, S., Moreau, H., Murreigh, H. et al. *The Silver Fairy Book*. London: Hutchinson and Co. (1895).

Farjeon, Eleanor. *The Silver Curlew*. Oxford Children's Library: Oxford University Press (1953).

Grimm, J. L. C. and W. C. *Grimm's Fairy Tales* (translated by Mrs Edgar Lucas). London: Constable & Company, Ltd (1909).

Lang, Andrew. *The Fairy Books* (Blue, Red, Green, Yellow, Crimson and Orange). Paternoster Road, London: Longmans, Green & Co. (1889–1906).

Perrault, Charles. *The Sleeping Beauty and Other Fairy Tales from the Old French* (retold by Arthur Quiller-Couch). London: Hodder and Stoughton (1912).

Tolkien, J. R. R. 'On Fairy-Stories', *Essays Presented to Charles Williams*. Oxford University Press (1947).